TESTAMENT

MARK P. DUNN

World Castle Publishing, LLC
Pensacola, Florida
Copyright © Mark P. Dunn 2018
Hardback ISBN: 9781629898551
Paperback ISBN: 9781629898568
eBook ISBN: 9781629898575
First Edition World Castle Publishing, LLC, January 15, 2018
http://www.worldcastlepublishing.com

Licensing Notes

Cover: Karen Fuller
Editor: Maxine Bringenberg

Table of Contents

PROLOGUE

My friend Steve Jones, who I had not seen or heard from in almost sixteen years, called me this morning and asked me meet him for a drink at his hotel. He was in town for an academic convention and would be staying at the Marriot by the airport, and he wanted to talk to me.

I said I would love to see him, and then asked him if anything was wrong. There was a silence on the other end of the line; in the background, I could hear faint noises of people talking, and then a PA announcement. I wondered what airport he was calling from.

"Steve?" I said, thinking the call may have been dropped. "Still there?"

"Yeah, man," he said, "still here. Let's just talk about it later, okay?"

When I hung up the phone, I walked into the kitchen, where Dottie was drinking a cup of coffee and picking around the edges of a slice of bread she'd burned in our prehistoric toaster-oven. She was scheduled to work a volunteer shift at the hospital later in the morning, and wore jeans and a rust-colored cardigan. Her brown hair, run through now with a few strands of dark gray, was back in a ponytail. She had one leg up on the chair and an elbow hooked around it. Through the window behind her I could see flurries drifting down onto the now-dormant garden patch, which in the spring and summer was a tempest of reds and oranges and yellows.

My fingers went absently to my right forearm and rubbed back and forth over the bumpy skin there, the result of a burn I'd suffered as a child. I realized what I was doing and stopped; when Dottie caught me at it, she always asked me if I wanted to talk, like I was trying to signal her that I was thinking about an issue I wasn't willing to bring up first. It was a habit that had started sometime in high school, and I still lapsed into it when my hands had nothing else to do, especially in social situations where all I wanted was a cigarette to fiddle around with.

"Who was that?" Dottie asked, looking up from the Sunday crossword puzzle in the *Inquirer*. She almost never wore makeup, and she didn't need it. Even at thirty-eight her face was remarkably unlined and youthful.

I shook my head, not exactly sure how to answer the question. Then I said, "Steve Jones, a friend from college. We're going to have a drink tonight at his hotel. He's in town. I just wanted to tell you I might not be here for dinner." My voice sounded toneless and fake in my ears, and I could feel a headache coming on.

"Steve Jones," she said, eyes going down as she thought. "Is that the guy from the farmhouse? The fire?"

"Yeah," I said. I couldn't remember all of what I'd told her about the fire, but I knew it wasn't the truth. Not the full truth, anyway.

"Okay," she said. "Maybe I'll take Naomi up to Manayunk for some pizza. She's been asking for a week. And I think she wants to go to Abercrombie or Banana Republic or one of those places. God knows what for."

The words came out before I even knew I'd thought them. "Don't let her buy anything trashy."

Dottie closed her eyes and breathed deeply, dropping her chin toward her chest. "She doesn't wear those kinds of things, Paul. She's not a trashy girl."

I was sorry I'd said anything at all. I knew Dottie was right and wanted to tell her so, but instead I said, "You know what I mean."

"This is about Nathan, I presume," Dottie said, shoving the crossword away from her. The pencil rolled off the paper and onto the wooden table, rattled its way to the edge, and dropped to the floor with a clatter.

"Look," I said, "I just—I don't know—I just don't want her to look like she's putting it out there, you know?"

"She's fifteen. Should I buy her a closet full of habits?"

"*Shit*, Dorothy, all I'm saying is I don't want her wearing jeans so tight I can see her ovaries. Let's leave a little mystery, okay?" I stood, breathing heavily, wondering how we had gotten here so quickly. "Maybe *I* should take her shopping next time."

Dottie stood up abruptly, and the backs of her knees sent the chair skittering backward over the tile floor of the kitchen. It teetered for a moment as though it would fall over backward, then butted up against the wall and clopped back down. "What the fuck is that supposed to mean?"

"I'm just saying that maybe she'd choose other clothes if it was me with her."

"Less slutty clothes is what you mean."

I threw up my hands. "Do you want me to spell it out?"

"You are *unbelievable* sometimes," she said. "That's your daughter!"

I couldn't stop it from coming. "That's exactly my point! Jesus *Christ!*"

Slowly, deliberately, Dottie bent over and picked up the pencil off the floor, then pulled her chair back to the table and sat down, dragged the crossword back toward her with a finger, and looked up at me. "Go for your run," she said. "We'll talk about this later."

For a long moment I stood there thinking about whether I wanted to say any of the things bubbling up my throat, but then I nodded and left, feeling hot and jerky in my body.

***

I pulled on an old pair of warm-ups, a light jacket, and my worn Reeboks and headed into the chilly morning, my mind lost in the fog that had blown in with Steve's call. The fight with Dottie had only intensified my feeling of confusion; when we fought, which was more often the longer we were together, I always felt like the ground had fallen away all around me, like I was standing on a narrow promontory, open air and jagged rocks around and beneath me.

The swimming, disoriented feeling took me back to the years after college, when I'd watched most of my days pass through this same milky, dizzy filter. Back then, the choice to remove myself from the world was voluntary, maybe even beneficial, but I didn't like the way it made me feel now, like I was setting foot back on a road that would take me nowhere I wanted to go. This was a temptation I'd once had to fight every day, but then I got a job and met Dorothy and we had Naomi, and the time I could dedicate to pursuing old memories dissipated like ground mist in the late morning sun.

I stretched quickly next to the garage, then broke into a jog at the bottom of the driveway, waiting for some sense of normality to set in. For the past ten years I'd been doing this, lacing up each day, whether before or after work, for what I jokingly called my "constitutional." Before running, it had been drinking; before that, in college, cigarettes and pot. It all worked out to the same, though. At some point each day, I needed a time to find my balance, and when I got home from a run, sweaty and tired, knees and ankles aching, I felt like I could be with my wife and my daughter. On days when there was no time to run, I knew I wasn't the same man.

After the first quarter mile, I picked up the pace. It was right around freezing and my breath huffed out white in front of me, then was buffeted away by the wind.

I wound my way through the streets of Wallingford and tried to concentrate on my breathing, the sound of my shoes padding on the ground. Usually this was the most peaceful time of my day, but today the sense of calm would not come. I kept replaying my argument with Dottie, wondering what I'd been thinking. Each time I thought of how I'd responded to her, a sour taste filled my mouth. I heard Steve's voice in my ear and felt again the way my stomach had dropped when I realized who it was, the way my mind had gone white and numb. My strides felt uneven and forced, and my breathing kept breaking rhythm, leaving me winded after only a mile.

I slowed to a walk and put my hands over my head to expand my lungs. I was on Martroy, a narrow street that wound its way along the Crum Creek, a tributary that twisted and turned its way through woods and civilization to the Delaware River. The creek had been a constant in my life since I was a kid, as had the woods. Back then you could eat the fish you caught in the Crum, and my friends and I had spent hours casting for small-mouth bass at the creek's wider points.

When Naomi was a little girl, we had come down here on summer days to look for garter snakes and box turtles sunning themselves on rocks that protruded from the shallows. We would catch them in a bucket, then bring them home and Naomi would keep them for a week or two, however long she could stand to hold them in captivity away from their families. She would go from rock to rock along the driveway, turning them for crickets and grubs to feed her pets, and she constructed elaborate twig and bark homes in the twenty-five gallon aquarium Dottie and

I purchased after weeks of begging. There would be plants and rocks transplanted from the creek, small branches for the snakes to twine themselves around. When she was ready, we would return to the exact same spot where we had captured the turtle or snake and free it, an act that always made her so happy. Because I was always so caught up in work and could barely find the time to accompany her to the creek, I never thought about how kind and humane a gesture it was from a girl of her age.

When she was old enough, she had stopped asking me to go along with her, and she would make the trip instead with her group of friends from the neighborhood. One of the boys, Nathan Greene, had stuck around longer than the others. Now he had become what could only be described as Naomi's first boyfriend, a development that scared me in a way simply beyond description. I knew what boys, even young ones, were capable of, had learned that lesson long ago. It wasn't something I liked to think about, but from time to time it bubbled to the surface when I wasn't ready. When those thoughts came, I tried to reassure myself that my experience was not the common one, but I didn't believe that, not really. Not in any part of me that mattered.

Up ahead there was an opening in the guard rails, and I walked between them and sat down on the frozen earth of the creek's bank, feeling like I was stuck on autopilot, not so much making choices as following imperatives launched forth from a remote center of my brain. The creek was still flowing, but had iced up around the bigger rocks that poked from the surface. Soon, I knew, the entire creek would be encased beneath a fragile layer of milky white. When I was a kid, I had always wondered how the fish lived during the winter, trapped under the ice with no air to breathe, how they could survive in the cold water, without the sun.

Before I knew it was coming, I started to cry.

At first I tried to stop it from happening, but it was useless.

10

I gave myself over and I sat there, my knees drawn up, elbows hooked over them, head down. Soon I started to hear their voices. Steve's. Roscoe's. Lucy's. Normally they were the voices that spoke to me when I ran, and only then; a long time ago, in the months and years after the fire at the farmhouse, their voices had been unwelcome, even cruel at times, constant companions. It had taken a long time to understand that I would never be rid of them, not completely, and even longer to build a place in my mind where they could live without destroying me. Now I heard them only when I shut everything else out, or when I'd neglected them for too long.

After a time a car zoomed by on the road behind me, and I realized that I had no idea how long I'd been sitting there. I stood up and brushed the dirt from my warm-ups, then headed back in the direction of the house, knees throbbing now from the cold. When I had loosened up a little, I broke into a slow jog, then picked up the pace.

This time my strides were long and sure, as if my time next to the Crum had steadied me. When I reached the house, I thought about continuing on, rounding the circuit once more. But then I thought of Dottie, thought of the shitty things I'd said, and decided that the voices would have to wait for the time being. I turned into the driveway, raising my arms and lacing my fingers together on top of my head, trying to breathe deeply.

***

When I walked through the front door of the Marriot at around six that evening, I wondered if I'd be able to recognize Steve after all this time. A thousand years ago Steve had been as grungy as any of us, his hair long and straight down to his shoulders, face alternately stubbly or clean-shaven, but always pale from too much time in Ohio. He was the kind of guy who, if he'd walked into a bar in Georgia or South Carolina or even parts of rural Pennsylvania, would have been met with bemused looks and maybe a few rumblings of "Hell, I don't know whether to fight him or fuck him." Back then, you had to be careful choosing a watering hole.

Thinking about those days, I was suddenly very aware of how my own appearance had changed. Long gone was the time when I'd worn torn jeans, peace sign T-shirts, and my hair down to my shoulders. Now I looked like most of the other men I knew in their late thirties. I earned decent money at the magazine — certainly more than I'd ever expected to earn with a degree in English — and I bought too much wine that Dottie and I liked to sit and drink on the back porch after Naomi had gone to bed, or when she was over at a friend's house for the night. The running had helped to keep some of the pounds off, but in the years since my freshman campaign at Penton College, my waist had gone from a 32 to a 36. Time and gravity had taken care of the rest, and for the first time in years I felt self-conscious about the lines on my face, the puffy bags underneath my eyes. Luggage, Dottie called them sometimes.

My hand went to my head, and I ran a hand over the sparse hair there; not dead yet, but hardly thriving. I felt a brief and ridiculous flare of hope that Steve looked worse, that the past decade-and-a-half had taken him farther from his youth than it had taken me.

Scattered around the dimly-lit space I saw clusters of men and women dressed in dark suits, most of them sipping drinks from tall glasses. These were the creatures who spent their days working in cubicles and offices in Center City, commuting an hour to and then another hour from work, seeing their families for dinner and maybe the duration of a sitcom or two, or an episode of *American Idol*, before falling asleep on the couch, exhausted, still wearing their work clothes. Before the age of the Internet, when it had been impossible to work from home, I'd been one of their number. I felt sad for them, and for their families who loved them but spent their days living with only the idea of a mom or dad.

In the far corner, near a plate window that overlooked a field between the hotel and the airport, I saw a lone man dressed in a white button-down shirt, his head sagging toward the table, the fingers of one hand holding a cigarette, the other running back and forth through his short-cropped, salt-and-pepper hair. Although I couldn't see his face, I knew it was Steve, and I felt an urge to turn around and leave before he saw me. Before I could make that choice, he looked up and raised the hand from his head in an uncertain wave.

He stood up and spread his arms, and I stepped into his hug.

"Paco," he said into my neck, squeezing me tightly.

"Hey, man," I said. In my embrace his body was skinny, almost emaciated, and I struggled to remember if he had always been that way. I didn't think so. He smelled like booze and smoke and something else, something more primal and cloying, from *within* him. It passed through my head suddenly that Steve wasn't here in Philadelphia for a conference at all, and it sent a bolt of fear through me that he might have come to this place from wherever he lived just to see me. I knew I didn't want to hear what he had to say.

We sat down on opposite sides of the small round table. Steve tapped ash from his cigarette and drew on it hard, and I could hear the paper crisp in the dry hotel air. He looked older than he was, and not by a little. If I didn't know better, I would have assumed he was fifty. His eyes traveled to the table and he saw my hands folded there.

"Married?" he said, smiling.

"For about fifteen years," I said. "You?"

Steve shook his head. "Tried for a while, but I wasn't very good at it. Kids?"

"One. Naomi."

13

"How old?"

"She's fifteen now." Even as I said the words, I wanted to take them back. What right did this man have to hear the intimate facts of my life? Whatever I had now I'd earned the hardest way; it had taken me the better part of my lifetime to get over the pain I'd suffered during the brief time Steve and I had been friends. I felt uncomfortable talking to him about my family, and I wanted him to stop asking me questions; I found that I was already calculating in my head how long I'd need to stay to avoid seeming rude. What was the point of this? Was I going to rekindle an old friendship after all this time? Come on.

"Damn," Steve said, shaking his head. "Can you believe how fast it goes by?"

"Time?"

"Life, man. A couple more years and your kid'll be in college."

"Scary enough to know they're out shopping right now."

Steve laughed and then asked me what I was doing for work. I told him that I was the City Section Editor of *Philadelphia Life* magazine and that the years had been good to me. Once or twice I let silences hang, hoping that Steve would volunteer something about himself, but he didn't. Instead he talked about college, about things we'd done, peripheral people we'd known. Never the main players, not Roscoe or Lucy. Instead he talked about our fraternity brothers, girls he'd slept with who were married now, the few people we'd both known in college who had died, mostly from cancer or car wrecks.

I nodded slowly as he talked, keeping my eyes on Steve's, still trying to figure out what he was doing. I considered and dismissed the possibility that he might be looking for money. Based solely on the clothes he was wearing, I could tell that he had done all right for himself. And if it was his intention to ask me for a loan, it hardly made sense that he would buy a plane ticket to fly out to see me. So, if not money, what? The potential answer was both the reason I had come here to meet Steve and the reason I almost hadn't.

For almost twenty years, I had operated on the assumption that blocking the past from my life was the only way to achieve any kind of normality, but that hadn't worked. My life was a ridiculous contradiction defined by a constant effort to both jettison the past and hold on to it. If I didn't figure out some way to cope with my own history, I was going to lose my family. Not tomorrow, and maybe not for years, but eventually. One day Dottie would realize, if she hadn't already, that I was never going to change, that the best she could ever hope for was the half of me not rooted firmly in the past.

Finally I said, "You said you were here for some kind of conference."

"Yeah," Steve said, then took a drink from his glass. "Not exactly."

Fighting the urge to shut my eyes or walk away, I said, "Why then?"

He tapped more ash into the ashtray then crushed his cigarette out, exhaling a plume of smoke as he did. I hadn't smoked since the end of college, but watching him made me want a cigarette badly. I decided against it. Three years ago I'd sat vigil beside my father's hospital bed in Riddle Memorial Hospital, and watched as the accordion-bag hooked to the life-support system stopped pumping air into his charred lungs. There are some trains you don't want to ride to the end of the line.

"Why?" he said, laughing softly to himself. "That's the question of the hour, isn't it?" Hearing my own thoughts echoed so closely in his words was disconcerting. His eyes dipped back toward the table, and I saw a sad smile spread across his face. "Nothing," he said. "I just wanted to see you, man. Will you stay for a while and just talk? It's been a long time since I've been able to do that with someone who would…you know, understand."

Part of me wanted to tell him I could only stay for a few minutes, that I had some kind of obligation later that night. But I didn't. And as Steve, my old friend, began to talk, I found myself remembering that first year of college, when everything had gone so right and then so very terribly wrong.

PART I

PENTON. ROSCOE BALLANTEMPS. A GIRL NAMED LUCY.

Chapter One

Late in August of 1985, my parents drove me to Philadelphia International Airport and put me on a plane to Ohio.

Why I chose Penton I still can't really say. I was a solid student, started for four years on the varsity basketball and baseball teams, and published short stories in my high school's literary magazine. I'd been accepted at most of the schools I applied to. At first, my mind was made up. Both of my parents had gone to school at Trinity in Hartford, and the college had taken on a certain mystique in my mind. Though I certainly never thought of it so clearly at the time, I imagine that, in my seventeen-year-old brain, going to college at Trinity meant living up to the standard my father and mother had set for me. Making my parents happy mattered very much, and whatever it took to make them proud, I would do it. But when the acceptance letter from Trinity came, my dad must have noticed something in my face.

"Paul," he said, sitting down across from me at the round, glass table in our kitchen. "That from Trinity?" He was smoking — my dad was *always* smoking — and looked tired. My father was a professor of engineering at Swarthmore College, and perpetually had a stack of papers a foot high piled on his desk. There were brownish-gray blotches under his eyes, the rims raw and red

18

from late nights spent sitting in his study correcting tests and labs.

"Yeah. Came today."

"Thought so."

I looked up at him, not knowing quite what he meant.

"You don't want to go there," he said. It was neither a question nor a statement, just a sentence. I let it hang, not because he wasn't right, but because there were so many things I thought I'd have to say in qualification. But I was wrong about that.

"It's okay," he said. "You'll be fine wherever you go. It's not where you go. It's what you do." He crushed out the cigarette in an elephant-shaped ceramic ashtray I'd made when I was a kid. "Where're you thinking? Not out to Iowa with the potato farmers, I hope."

There was nothing in his voice that signaled disappointment, anger, frustration. In the way you can only do with people you love so well that you never really think about it, I knew with certainty that my father was giving me an unconditional release from the guilt I'd been preparing myself to feel. I felt a weight lift that I hadn't even realized I was carrying.

"Do you remember Penton?" I asked. We'd taken a whirlwind tour of the Ohio schools the previous spring, and though my recollection was a little fuzzy, I remembered that Penton was small and intimate, within walking distance of a working-class town, and that several members of the English Department faculty were younger and more progressive than their counterparts at the other schools we'd toured. I couldn't picture specific dormitories or the academic buildings, but those details tended to swim together after touring five or six campuses in a couple of days. I had an overall impression of stone and brick, a feeling of history.

"How sure are you?" he said.

"Pretty sure. Do you think Mom'll be okay with that?"

My father smiled and tapped another Camel from the pack

that always rode shotgun in his breast pocket. "She'll be fine with it."

She had been, and five months later I woke from a fitful doze as the plane set down in Columbus.

***

My roommate freshman year was a guy named Roscoe Ballantemps, from a small town not too far from Pittsburgh.

A couple of weeks after my father had sent in the deposit to hold my spot at Penton, a letter arrived containing my housing assignment. At the bottom of the form was a paragraph suggesting that I get in touch with my roommate, the very thought of which closed my throat and dried my mouth. I'd been away from home before, a week or two at camp, but those had always been decidedly unpleasant experiences I equated with sleepless nights listening to muffled farts, coughing, and crying. As much as I was looking forward to college, I dreaded the thought of living with another person. I didn't want to share a bathroom or deal with someone else's personal problems or clean up any mess I didn't make.

For almost two months I'd put off making the call, but there was nothing to be done about it, and my mother finally cornered me one weekend not long before I was scheduled to leave. The woman who answered the phone sounded drunk and irritated. I identified myself and asked for Roscoe. I'd never known someone named Roscoe before, but to me it sounded country, like trouble. By the time he finally got to the phone several minutes later, I'd made a number of initial assumptions about the whole family.

"Yeah," a phlegm-clotted voice said. I heard the sound of throat clearing, hocking, and then spitting. When the voice spoke again, it said, "Yeah."

"Hi, this is Paul Callahan," I said. "Your roommate next year."

"Is there a problem or something?"

"I'm sorry?"

"Is there a problem, I said. Do you need to talk to me about something?" He sounded preoccupied and completely disinterested.

I thought about how to respond. "Uh, no. Just wanted to touch base. We're supposed to talk about what we're each bringing, you know, for the room."

More throat clearing, the sound of another loogie being launched. I wondered if he was inside, and if the spit was going onto the floor or into a cup or something, then grimaced at the image. "Don't worry about that," Roscoe said. "Got it covered."

"Are you sure?" I said. "I can bring a small TV, and I've got a stereo. I don't know if—"

"Look," Roscoe said, "I'm kind of in the middle of something right now."

"Yeah, okay. Should I give you a call ba—"

I heard a click and thought for a moment that Roscoe had dropped the phone, but then the dial tone hummed into life and I hung up.

"Great," I said to my bedroom. "Just wonderful."

***

The first time I met Roscoe, things didn't go any better.

I took a cab from Columbus International Airport to Smith Hall, a blocky brick structure three stories high, a small dining hall growing out of its side. It looked more like a hospital, I thought, than a place where people lived. Most of the previous night I'd spent with friends from high school at a group going-away party, and I was exhausted, my head throbbing from fatigue, my eyes gritty and dry. As a general rule, I didn't drink, but I'd indulged in a couple of beers and had the first hangover of my life. I wasn't doing very well emotionally, either, which I hadn't anticipated.

For the better part of the last year I'd been dating a girl named Josephine Collins. I'd known her since the third grade, when her family had moved into a house a couple of streets over, but we'd never been anything more than friends until a Christmas party both of our parents had dragged us to. We were the only two people at the party under thirty, and had spent the entire night together. When I called her a couple of days later to grab some pizza downtown, she'd said yes. I can still remember the tone of her voice; she seemed to feel the same as me, like she'd finally found someone she could just be herself with.

Jo was pretty and smarter by degrees than the other girls in our class. The day after I left for Penton, she was headed to Colby College in Maine, and we had agreed that carrying on with a long-distance relationship would be a mistake. Both of us had friends who had tried to keep things going when their significant others headed off to college, and the effort never seemed to bring them anything but pain. But sitting with Jo on a bench on the back deck of Larry Wilson's house, the party carrying on loud and raucous inside, both of us teared up. Later, we'd gone back to my house and spent the rest of the night lying on the couch in the basement.

At one point, as I was just dozing off, Jo whispered, "I love you, you know." Her hands were resting on my forearms, and she brushed her thumb gently over the pebbly network of burn scars there. It was a gesture that said, *I know you, know everything about you, the good and the bad.* And that was true. Jo knew me better than anyone.

"I love you, too." It wasn't the first time we'd said the words to each other, and I always meant them, but this time they were more for comfort than anything else. "We're doing the right thing, Jo. Don't you think?"

I felt her nod her head, then she whispered, "It's all going to change."

I opened my eyes. Our foreheads were nearly touching, our hands wrapped together beneath our chins. "What is?"

"Everything." She paused and I thought she would say something else. Instead she just said, "Everything."

We both finally drifted off to sleep, and it was my mother calling down from the kitchen a couple of hours later that woke us up. When I walked Jo back to her house and said goodbye, there were no tears; both of us were out.

In the bathroom at the Columbus airport I'd looked at my reflection in a mirror and actually groaned at the haggard face staring back at me, bloodshot and unshaven. I felt like at any moment I might burst into tears from the weight of the unfocused sadness sitting on my chest, and I knew I must look that way, too. In a way I couldn't put into an order that made sense, I missed Jo, missed the feeling inside of me that she stood for. On top of that, I was hung over and felt like a skin of putrid oil was sitting on top of everything in my stomach. But there was something else, too, something I didn't understand at the time. I felt desperate, panicky. Everything was moving too fast, and it was all out of my control. I knew my feelings were written on my face; just the way I wanted to come across on my first day at college. Trying to hold myself together, feeling lonely and adrift, I made my way out to the cab line and waited for my turn.

After signing in at Smith Hall, I climbed the three flights to the top floor. All I wanted was to lie down on a mattress — hell, the *floor* would do — and sleep for roughly a week. I was emotionally spent, and although I had managed to convince myself that I was totally prepared to leave home, I had to choke back tears again and again and fight the lump that kept building in my throat.

Sleep, I thought, opening the stairwell door and stepping onto the third floor of Smith Hall. *A little sleep will make it all okay.*

A long hall, the walls painted white with a red stripe running horizontally, stretched off in front of me. The carpet was a faded orange and yellow pattern, and when I looked down I could see cigarette burns scorched into the pile. The walls were covered with posters and notices, and more had slumped off the wall and onto the floor.

An image of my house back in Swarthmore flitted into my head — my neat room, the kitchen with its smells of rosemary and basil and fresh coffee; the living room, where I sat and watched Phillies and Sixers games with my dad — and I knew I was going to break down soon, could feel it bubbling up in my stomach and throat and behind my eyes. I swallowed and took a deep breath, and shook my head to clear it.

There weren't many students around yet — I'd arrived two days early because my parents were going to visit my mother's sister in Florida — but a few representatives of each gender wandered in and out of rooms, most of them with bottles of beer in their hands, wearing torn jeans and T-shirts. A couple of them glanced at me and then away again, uninterested. What was I to them? Just another newbie. They didn't know me, didn't know anything about who I was, or care for that matter.

Someone was playing Billy Joel's "Piano Man" too loud somewhere down one of the hallways, and I could smell the sweet odor of pot in the air. I hefted my bags and headed down the hall as I'd been directed.

When I found my room I unlocked it and stepped inside. I had fully expected to be the first one in the room, but I wasn't. Nor was I the second.

In front of me, obscuring the window, a set of gray, metal bunk beds shifted and squeaked. The bottom bunk was empty. The top was a heaving and jerking pile of blanket and human flesh. I could see a foot jutting up, its big toe tapping the ceiling in rhythm with the motion of the bunk. As I stood in the open doorway, lost in some nether region of indecision, one of the two people under the blanket reached critical mass and yelled out, "Fuck yes!"

The bed stopped moving and the foot wilted, and for perhaps

three breathless seconds I waited. Whether I was waiting for the blanket to be thrown back or for someone to jerk me out of the doorway from behind, I didn't know. But a head emerged and looked at me. When I heard the voice, I knew it was Roscoe.

"Hey, man. Come on in."

I dropped my bags on the floor and stood where I was.

I heard a female voice say quietly, "Who's there?"

Roscoe sat up, swung his legs over the side of the bed, and dropped to the floor, completely naked, still half at attention. He was about my height, six feet tall, his hair brown and long, down to his shoulders. A wispy beard covered the lower half of his face. He took a couple of steps forward, winked at me, then gestured behind himself with a thumb, and said, "She's still hot if you want a turn."

"That's okay," I said, managing to find my voice at last.

"Suit yourself," he said, then called out over his shoulder, "Hey, want to take a shower?"

"Absolutely," the girl said, throwing off the blanket, baring her naked body. My eyes still hadn't adapted well enough to the dark to see much, but I got an impression of something large and pale and blonde.

I felt my face go hot and turned away as she climbed down from the bed. A minute later I heard the shower spring to life, and then the sound of the shower door.

In my mind I went as quickly as I could back to the basement with Jo, her cool hand on my forearm, sleep coming to us both, my safe, cozy house at rest above us. I dropped my bags on the bottom bunk and left the room to find a place to wait until the room was empty.

CHAPTER TWO

By the end of my first two weeks at Penton, a few things had become clear to me. One was that no matter how hard I tried to avoid it, my world view was going to be compromised in ways I couldn't even begin to predict. Already I'd walked in on Roscoe three times while he was atop or behind or underneath some girl or other. And worse, seeing the girls with whom Roscoe was engaged encompassed the totality of my experience with actual sex. Jo and I had always been comfortable with each other, but neither of us had been interested in taking things too far too fast; the furthest we'd ever gone was an extended grope-session, culminated by a dry and somewhat painful handjob in the back of my dad's Bonneville. Each time I came back to the room and found Roscoe going at it, I'd turned around and headed back out for fresh air, coffee, and time to sort out what was a strange contradiction of feelings inside of me.

On one hand, he was repulsive. The way he looked was a big part of the reason, but it was only a starting point. He wore his brown hair long and unkempt most of the time, often down over his face, which was nearly Cro-Magnon in its construction. Low, prominent brow. Sparse facial hair that would never progress into a true beard, but which he let grow long and ragged nonetheless.

Jeans, always the same pair, ripped in the crotch and about fifteen other places, and whatever yellow-pitted shirts he found in his laundry basket. I'd frequently seen him giving his clothing what he called the "smell test" before he put it on, but I'd never seen an item fail. I didn't know why he even bothered.

His exploits with the opposite sex were another matter altogether. Though I hadn't gotten a good look at the girl that first night, I'd seen more than I wanted of the last three, each of whom had been fat, ugly, or both...not that this kept them from shedding their clothing at the drop of a hat. Something about Roscoe's acts of promiscuity wrenched the part of me that believed in the essential morality of the world. It's not that I was planning to wait for marriage before having sex, but there had to be *something*, didn't there?

Not for Roscoe.

What bothered me, though, and what kept me out walking the Penton campus late at night instead of returning to the room, was that, even in those early weeks, I knew part of me envied Roscoe. That in some place deep inside of myself, I wanted to do the things he did.

I had talked to Jo on the phone a few times since arriving at Penton, but each time there was a strange formality to what we said; there were too many protracted silences. Our shorthand had lapsed, and we were just two people on the phone with five hundred miles between us. Behind her I could always hear people talking, and though she never told me she needed to go, I knew she wanted to. I felt both happy for her and jealous. I wanted the same things, and Roscoe seemed to stand for *living*. At times I wanted to tag along with him when he went out at night, but those urges were always quashed by a sense that doing so would only lead to a kind of trouble I wouldn't know how to handle. I was sure he spent his nights up on the Hill, making rounds at the fraternity houses, hanging out with brothers who drank too much and got into fights over girls or cards or any number of other things; maybe he even went down to the bars on Sandusky Street with his new friends. Who knew? Roscoe and I couldn't have been more different.

But what *really* bothered me, what scared me horribly, was that I liked him. Never in my life had I met someone more charismatic. Even when he was being crass or rude, and he was *usually* being crass and rude, Roscoe possessed the raw kind of magnetism that most people worked and worked for but could never pull off. People loved Roscoe. Girls. Guys. It didn't matter.

On Friday of our first week together, Roscoe barged into the room, slamming the door into the wall, eyes frantic, long hair tied back in a loose ponytail tied off with a piece of twine.

"Paul, get dressed," he said, throwing his knapsack on the floor. "We're going out, you pussy."

I'd been reading Ovid's *Metamorphoses*, feet up on my desk, a cup of the bitter coffee from the student union cradled in my lap. The radio was on to some news program and the DJ was talking about the French bombing of *The Rainbow Warrior*, railing against the snooty environmentalists from Greenpeace. Roscoe snapped the radio off and stood there expectantly, looking down at me.

"It's a school night," I said, and hated the sound of my words even as I said them. Jo wasn't up in Maine telling her friends that she couldn't go out tonight; she was doing what we'd agreed we would do, taking advantage of being away from home, away from her parents, away from me.

"You fag," Roscoe said, but he was smiling, and not cruelly or angrily. He looked like a parent whose child had just declared that they would *not* eat their lima beans. "You fucking *fag*. Put that book down and come with me. You won't regret it. I promise."

"Where do you want to go?"

"Just come with me, man. We've been living together for a week and you've barely left the room. That's fucking sad. People keep asking if I live with a shut-in or something. Really, I *want* you to come. Don't make me beg."

And against my every instinct, I went.

Chapter Three

The day after I arrived in Ohio, a sweltering hot spell began, and now, weeks after I'd arrived, it still hadn't let up. Everywhere I went, people were talking about the heat, the humidity, complaining about the lack of air-conditioners in the dorms and classrooms. I showered before I went to class and then again when I got home in the evening, then spent the rest of the night in front of the oscillating fan, cold cans of Dr. Pepper from the mini fridge propped between the chair and the back of my neck. All of my books had bloated and warped from the humidity, and when I stood up, I had to peel myself out of chairs and check my pants in the bathroom for embarrassing sweat lines.

Earlier in the week I had seen a bright yellow notice on the bulletin board in Sturges Hall, the word WARNING printed in block letters across the top. It was an advisory from the local police to be on the lookout for rabid dogs. Apparently the heat was taking its toll on more than just the human population. The local powers-that-be had also placed restrictions on water usage, and every lawn in Penton was sun-browned and crispy.

The night Roscoe took me out was the worst yet. A layer of thick, bruised clouds hovered over the Ohio flatness, and from time to time a wet peal of thunder announced its presence from miles off. Everyone was waiting for the storm that would bring cooler air. And everyone was sure that when it finally did arrive, it would be one high-toned mother.

As we stepped outside, the air I pulled into my lungs felt like wet cotton.

"Jesus," Roscoe said. "It's like fucking Cambodia out here." He pulled a pack of cigarettes from the breast pocket of his Hawaiian shirt and lit one, sucked smoke, and blew it out through his nose like a dragon. I wasn't a big fan of cigarettes to begin with, but I wondered how smoking one on a day like this could possibly bring anyone pleasure.

"Where to?" I asked, already regretting my decision to come along on this little field trip. Sweat beaded on my forehead and ran down my temples and into my eyes. I already had an exit plan brewing, could practically see myself slapping my forehead and saying *Shit, man. I totally forgot about that paper for* Myth, Legend and Folklore. *Sorry, I gotta go back to the room....*

Roscoe pointed toward town. I fell in beside him and we walked along Spring Street in silence, making our way into Penton and then through it. We passed Rutherford's, a tiny two-aisle establishment that was the town's only bookstore, and then The West End and the Backstretch, bars so run-down they looked like they'd been there before the rest of the town rose up around them.

The town was nothing like what I'd expected it to be when I decided to come here. Penton wasn't quaint at all, for one thing; instead, it was unabashedly blue-collar, full of overworked stiffs and farmers who would just as soon run you over as honk at you to get out of the road. My second day at school, I'd been crossing Sandusky Street when the light turned yellow. A black Camaro gunned its engine and jumped toward me so fast I barely made the other side of the road, and as it thundered away down the road, I could clearly hear the sound of laughter.

Based on what I'd seen so far, that just seemed to be Penton. The townies hated the students, the students looked at the townies like freaks in a circus sideshow, and the professors occupied a sort of middle-ground, permanent cogs in the community, but not *of* the community. All in all, the final result was a kind of perpetual tension between groups of people who made each others' lives possible.

Even though it was only eight o'clock, there were few people out on the street. Since the heat wave started, Penton's population had been spending as little time outside as possible, preferring to while the time away in front of their window AC units or, for those who couldn't afford such a luxury, buckets of ice full-up with steel cans of Pabst Blue Ribbon or Natural Pilsner. A few of the professors even kept ice-buckets by their desks during class.

"Can I ask you a question?" Roscoe said as we crossed Sandusky Street and continued down Spring, headed now for the residential side of town.

"Okay."

"Do you think I'm a pig?"

"What do you mean?"

"You know, the girls, the booze, the smokes. I just want to know where we stand." He plugged his cigarette into his mouth and focused on adjusting his ponytail, which, sodden with moisture, had come loose in places. There were gray stains at his armpits and on the collar of his shirt.

"I'd be lying if I said I understand everything you do," I said, trying to figure out how to say something that was true but not *totally* true. I started to add something else, then stopped.

"What?" he said. "What were you going to say?"

We'd come to the stubby concrete bridge that crossed the brown trickle of the Olentangy River, and Roscoe stopped halfway across and leaned his elbows against the rail. I stood next to him and looked out over the murky water, the level of which had dropped by nearly a foot since the hot spell began. An empty cardboard milk carton and two beer cans butted up against a big rock and twisted in an eddy. I watched for a moment, then turned back to Roscoe.

"Why do you do it?"

He thought for a second, then said, "Pussy's pussy, know what I mean?"

"Not really."

"Not really about pussy being pussy, or not really about knowing what I mean?"

"Both."

Roscoe flicked the butt of his cigarette into the water and it floated slowly downstream. "Way I see it," he said, "I have a good time, they have a good time. So you feel like taking a bath in bleach when you wake up in the morning. I can live with that."

I didn't say anything because I didn't have any words to offer. We were so different from one another we could almost have been from different planets, and even though Roscoe and I were the same age, I felt young and inexperienced and inadequate.

Roscoe lit another cigarette and started walking again, apparently satisfied with my inability or unwillingness to respond, but what he'd said made a kind of sense to me I didn't want to admit. This was what Roscoe did. He made me wonder why I hadn't pushed Jo for sex, and made me feel like there might be something wrong with *me* for not having done so. He made me feel like I was defective somehow for not going out with him at night looking for something warm to bring back to the room, like I was missing the point of my life in some way, and I didn't know what to do with that, either.

We left the bridge and passed into a residential neighborhood. On both sides of the street, modest houses sat behind square lawns, all of which were well-manicured if sunburned. In my limited experience with Ohio, this type of house had come to

33

define the state. Simple. Neat.

The houses in Swarthmore were nothing like these. Most of the homes in my town were set well back from the road, separated from the constant passage of traffic by sprawling lawns, wandering driveways bordered by old railroad ties, and lines of elm and oak trees. Since the college was an arboretum, every square inch of the grounds was occupied by some variety of tree or shrub or flower.

My parents' house, once the home of the college dean, was bordered on one side by a thicket of rhododendrons, on another by a copse of old elms. A gigantic sycamore, ten feet around the trunk, dominated the sloping backyard, and in the summer honeysuckle grew in sweet-smelling tangles all over the trellis my mother had put up when she and my father bought the house. When I was a child, my mother showed me how to pluck the stamen from the bottom of the flowers to get to the nectar. A memory came to me then, so powerful and clear that I nearly had to stop walking. It was of me and my mother when I was seven or eight, sitting together on the wooden picnic table in the backyard near the honeysuckle vines, churning a batch of homemade ice-cream. The sky was a bright and flawless blue, the brick of the house a rich, baked red, green grass, me and my mother, younger and laughing.

A surge of depression, black and irrefutable, swept over me, and it was all I could do to keep my feet moving. What was I doing here? Why had I come? With my father a professor in the engineering department at the college, I would have been accepted at Swarthmore. Why hadn't I applied? Why had I chosen to travel five hundred miles away, to the godforsaken middle of nowhere, where I knew nobody except my pervert of a roommate, where I felt out of place and lost? I should have gone to Swarthmore, or if not there, then Haverford or Villanova. This had been a bad, stupid choice, and I resolved to find out how I could start the transfer process as quickly as possible. Maybe I could get in by next semester. If I had to spend one more here, I didn't—

"You ever been laid?"

"That's none of your goddamned business." The words came out as though I'd already been preparing to say them.

"Touchy, touchy, Paco. I take it that's a no."

"So what? Does that make me some kind of pariah or something?" Even as I asked the question, I realized how accurately I'd just described the way I felt.

"No," Roscoe said, "It just makes you funny to me. I'll probably make fun of you a lot. Don't worry, we'll get you some boom-boom."

"No thanks," I said.

I expected some kind of rejoinder, but instead Roscoe stopped and said, "We're here."

***

"Here" turned out to be the mouth of a cracked driveway bracketed by crumbling ten-foot brick walls. Dead ivy snaked its way up the brick and over the rounded top.

On both sides of the driveway, elm trees towered, their branches hiding the sky. So thick was the canopy that I almost felt as though I was walking through a high-vaulted interior passageway. The cover also served to obscure the house until we were almost upon it.

"Pretty cool, huh?" Roscoe said, turning back to me.

Though that wasn't the word I would have used, the house—or more accurately, the *mansion*—was impressive. Even in its derelict state, I could see what the place once must have been.

The façade was wide, and peeling columns flanked the double-doors. Half of the windows were broken, and the ones that weren't had taken on a permanently fogged appearance, but it was easy to see that once, a long time ago, this house had been the grandest on the block…on any block in this town, for that matter. I wondered why it was abandoned now, why it had apparently been so for some time. All I could think of was that something horrible must have happened here. It was a discomfiting feeling, and if there was one thing I knew, it was that I didn't want to go inside.

"Who's in there?" I asked. This all had the feel of some bizarre initiation rite into something I didn't want to be a part of.

"Don't know," Roscoe said. "One of the brothers at Sigma Theta told me about it." He grinned and started toward the door. From inside I could hear the faint sound of music.

"Wait," I said.

Roscoe stopped and looked back at me. "What? Afraid you might have a good time? Come on."

CHAPTER FOUR

The door was slightly ajar, and I could hear music coming from somewhere deep inside the house. I knew the place was probably condemned, and that if the cops showed up we'd be screwed, but the house was set far back from the road. Unless someone actually called the police to complain, they'd never know anyone was here.

The darkened foyer smelled stale and musty. I didn't know how long a house had to sit empty for an odor like that to develop, but I had begun to think that the house had been empty not just for years, but for decades.

My eyes adjusted slowly to the dim light, and I could see cracked black and white checkerboard tile beneath my feet. The paint on the walls had peeled away in long strips, and there were dried leaves and crumpled wads of newspaper scattered on the floor. Here and there, leftover furniture covered by sheets hulked in the shadows.

"Roscoe!" A guy's voice snapped me out of myself and I registered the world around me again. Just a few feet ahead of me, Roscoe was shaking someone's hand.

"Hey, Steve," I heard Roscoe say. "This is Paul. The one I was telling you guys about."

A dark shape loomed in front of me and I put my hand out, and got one of those handshakes where the "hard" is the point, not the shake.

"Good to meet you, man," the guy said, and clapped my shoulder with his free hand. "Come on in. Let's get you boys some brew."

We followed Steve into the heart of the house, a large, high-domed room that was probably thirty feet wide. Lit candles, dozens of them, filled every available flat surface, light enough to reveal the space around us.

The walls, once white, were now a grainy yellow, and squared with the ghosts of pictures no longer hung. There was no furniture, but blankets had been spread on the floor. A silver keg sat in a trough of ice, and there were also a couple of plastic coolers full of canned beer near the blankets. Empties littered the corners of the room.

There were no windows and the acoustics were fantastic. I could hear two girls whispering near the beer keg, another guy talking to his friend near the door. I thought that maybe this had been a music room at one time. Someone had brought a boom-box along, and the Allman Brothers' "Midnight Rider" was playing.

"Fuck yeah," Roscoe said. "This is the joint, man."

"Just keep it quiet around school," Steve said. "Last thing we need is the cops all over the place."

"How did you find it?" I asked him.

"One of the seniors at Sig Theta showed a bunch of us when we were pledges. I guess it's been a house tradition for years."

We walked to the keg and Steve drew us each a cup of beer, then said, "Want to meet some girls?"

"You know it, man," Roscoe said, and laughed. He looked over at me briefly, then said to Steve, "He does, too. He just doesn't know it yet. He's a virgin."

I didn't say anything, but I felt something flip over in my

bowels like a fish. This was what I had asked for; this was why I should have stayed back in the room. I looked away and tried to pretend I didn't feel angry.

"Then let's go." Steve led us over to one of the blankets, where five people were sitting. "Hey, I've got a couple of guys I'd like you to meet," he said, and the people on the blanket looked up.

And that's when I saw her.

**

She was a small, slender girl, almost waifish, and wore her long, wavy brown hair down over her shoulders, a few loose strands of hair sticking to the side of her damp neck, the underside of her chin. In a few places she'd woven purple and white wildflowers into it. As I watched, she reached up and replaced one that had come loose, twining strands of hair into place until it was fixed.

She wore old jeans that were torn at both knees, and a gray T-shirt with the words JOE'S GOOD EATS stenciled across the front in faded maroon lettering. Underneath the shirt I could read the suggestion of her body, but even though my eyes had adjusted to the dim lighting for the most part, I couldn't see as much as I wanted to.

She was one of those ethereal girls you see sometimes at parties, slipping in and out of different crowds, able to fit in anywhere but at home nowhere. I realized that I was staring and tore my eyes off her. There were two guys beside Steve, Roscoe, and myself, and two girls sat together near the girl in the gray shirt and torn jeans, occasionally leaning over to whisper in each others' ears. I saw immediately that the girl I'd first noticed wasn't really one of their crowd. She had been accepted but not taken in. I wondered how anyone could *not* be looking at her.

Steve introduced us around and we sat, Roscoe near the girls, me near the wall. I sipped my beer, not really tasting it, and stared at the girl, unable to stop myself.

39

One of the girls, a blonde wearing a tie-dyed shirt with a red peace sign in the middle, said, "We were thinking about a game."

"What game?" one of the other guys asked. He was scrawny and cave-chested, and his dark beard hung long and dirty-looking against the breast of an equally ratty tan linen shirt.

She shot him a look, and I could tell immediately that there was some tense history there. "I don't know. Maybe Spin the Bottle, *Jerome*. Maybe you want to suck on *Mandy's* face some more. How's that sound?"

"Come on, baby," he said. "I don't want to fight tonight."

"No," Steve said. "Something else. Last time we played Spin the Bottle I ended up lip-locked with Dan all night."

"In your wildest fucking dreams," the other guy said, and then belched.

"Okay," Steve said. "How about breaking into the penalty box?"

"I'm *about* that," the big guy said. The girls rolled their eyes.

***

The penalty box turned out to be a hallway closet just outside the music room door.

"What's going on?" I asked Roscoe. Behind us I could hear the faint sounds of music and talking, but even a few feet outside of the big room, we seemed to be miles away.

"Dunno," he said. "But if it involves beer, girls, or both, I'm all about this shit." He looked at me urgently, then leaned closer. "Just go with it, Paco. You only live once, know what I'm saying?"

Stopping in front of the closet, Steve turned back to the eight of us standing in the dark corridor. Though my eyes were on him, I felt something brush against my arm and looked down. The girl was there, even slighter and smaller than I'd thought at first. She turned her eyes up at me and the corners of her mouth lifted in a smile. I felt my face try to respond and fail. Then, thankfully, Steve spoke.

"This," he said, and in the dim light of the candles a couple of the girls had brought along, I saw him gesture at the door on his left, "is the Penalty Box. In a time-honored tradition, we will now do our goddamn best to suck down an unholy amount of beer and cigarette smoke in as little time as possible." He opened the door, and I saw that someone had tacked index cards to the wood.

"What are those?" Roscoe asked, squinting at the door.

"Record times," Steve said. He pointed at one of the three vertical columns of cards. "There are three categories. Guy with guy, guy with girl, and girl with girl."

Roscoe now began to look slightly nervous. "Guy with guy?"

"Nothing like that," Steve said. "Don't worry."

"Naughty boy," Tie-dye said.

"So what are the teams then?" Roscoe asked.

"We have even numbers," Steve answered. "Let's go guy-girl."

"Awesome," Tie-dye said, and slipped her arm through Steve's.

One of the other girls latched onto the mammoth with the vein-popped arms, and I saw Roscoe standing with his arm around a short, chunky brunette.

Which left me with....

I looked down at the girl, who hadn't moved from my side. She was looking straight ahead at the closet door, but I felt her hand settle on my wrist, soft and dry, barely a presence there.

We chose the order by picking numbers between one and ten.

"Five," Roscoe said. His eyes were eager, and as I watched, his hand settled on the brunette's back and traced its way slowly down toward her ass before settling on the substantial shelf that marked its beginning. She didn't seem to mind.

"Three," said the mammoth.

41

"Ten," Jerome said. His partner, a tall, thin blonde, had an arm wrapped around his waist. Jerome appeared to have forgotten about Tie-dye for the time being.

When it came to us, the girl said, "One."

Tie-dye chose for herself and Steve. "Seven."

After a moment's thought, Steve said, "The number was one, so the order is Paul and Lucy, Dan and Paula, Roscoe and Jeanette, me and Carla, and then Jerome and Mandy. Each team will go into the closet with six beers and six cigarettes. Fastest team to finish gets to make one rule that will last the rest of the year."

"Any rule?" Lucy asked, and her fluid voice was tinged with a sly tone. Her hand still hadn't moved from my arm. In fact, she seemed almost preternaturally still. A few moments from now I would enter the closet with her. Panic clenched in my gut and I thought of Jo, thought to myself, *what would she think if she knew I was doing this?* and then shook my head to clear it, trying to think about nothing. A series of words ran through my brain, then rounded the turn and passed through again and again. *This isn't me this isn't me this isn't me....*

"Anything," Steve answered. "Last year, we had four winners. One made the rule that whenever he said, we had to drop our pants. No matter where we were." He smiled, remembering. "The asshole was in my Cultural Anthropology class. I won't give too many details, but suffice it to say, the final exam was a train wreck. Glad I wore underwear that day."

Lucy nodded, a smile tugging gently at one side of her mouth. "Okay."

Someone had dragged a plastic cooler into the hallway, and now Steve went to it, flipped the top back, and started pulling out steel cans of Pabst Blue Ribbon. He handed me three cans and gave Lucy the other three, then turned to the others and said, "Now we need butts. Ante up."

Roscoe pulled a pack out of his pocket and tapped six cigarettes into his hand, then handed them to me, dropping me a wink as he did so.

"Ready, you two?" Steve asked.

"Almost," Lucy said. "I just have one question. What's the record?"

Grinning, Steve said, "One minute and thirty-seven seconds. Steve Jones, class of nineteen eighty-six, and Sasha Simonini, class of nineteen eighty-four. She graduated last year, but Christ could that girl drink some beer." He tapped a note card with a finger. "I don't think this card will be going anywhere anytime soon. Enough of this bullshitting. You two ready?"

Chapter Five

There are spans of time in your life that you never forget, moments that keep working in your brain even when you're not aware of it. My three and a half minutes in the closet of the abandoned house with Lucy were like that.

In the almost twenty years since then, I've woken hundreds of times during the night with her smell in my nose, the feel of her hands on my body. I've found myself drifting off at work, or in my quiet times at home, completely lost, snapping back to the present in front of my computer or staring out a window at nothing.

It started with Steve ushering us into the closet, which was cramped, our backs pressed up against shelving. Lucy divvied three of the beers and three of the cigarettes into clusters for each of us and set the matchbook down on the middle shelf. I looked back at Steve, feeling uncertain.

Something in his face unsettled me, but it was hard to put a tag on what that thing was. Maybe he was scared, though that made no real sense on its own. Mixed with it was something else. Jealousy. Concern. I couldn't really tell, but then it was gone as he reached some kind of conclusion inside his own mind.

"Rules are these, bitches," he said. "No shotgunning. If there are any holes in the cans, you'll be disqualified. The cigarettes have to be smoked down to the butt, and don't even think about ripping the tops off and putting them in your pocket. Comprende?"

I nodded and Lucy said, "Yup."

"Then let's do this thing. May the best man and woman win." He smiled broadly, then added, "And I guarantee you that *we* will."

For a second I was looking out at everyone standing there, framed in the doorway like a still-life portrait, then Steve checked his watch, counted down from five, and closed the door.

***

The darkness was almost complete, the only light coming from the crack underneath the door. Then I heard the scratch of a match and yellow light flared into life.

Lucy lit a cigarette and handed it to me. "Here," she said. "Don't inhale. Just puff. Otherwise you'll get sick." She lit another for herself and cracked a beer. I did likewise and took a deep swallow. The beer tasted bitter and skunky, but at least it was cold. The last time I'd had a beer was the night before getting on the plane to come here, and I thought of Jo again, sitting with her on Larry Wilson's back deck, my arm over her shoulders.

I heard Lucy belch softly and then giggle to herself, then the sound of an empty can being dropped on the floor. A moment later, I heard the hiss-pop of another top.

"Jesus," I said. "I can't keep up with you." As soon as I spoke, I hated the words. *Stupid*, I told myself. *Shut up. Just drink.* I tipped the can back and let the beer slide down my throat. When I was done, I dropped the can on the floor, groped in the darkness for another, found it, and opened it. I could feel the cold beer swimming in my stomach.

"Good boy," Lucy said. "There's hope for you yet."

I realized that I'd been ignoring my cigarette. By mistake I inhaled and found myself coughing, but managed to stop. From outside the door I heard the sound of Roscoe laughing, and wished him a nice room in hell.

There was another flare of yellow light and for a moment I saw Lucy's face as she lit two more cigarettes at the same time. She handed both to me and said, "Smoke these." She turned to the door and called out, "Time!"

A second later, Steve's voice came back. "Two minutes and twelve seconds. What the hell are you guys doing in there, anyway? Origami?"

There was more laughter and I heard Roscoe say, "He just needs some breaking in, that's all. Give me a little time."

In the last light of the guttering match, I saw Lucy smile. "Oh well," she said. "We can't win. Steve and Clara won't take more than two minutes." The match went out and we were back in the darkness.

I pulled on both of the cigarettes at once, and then asked around a mouthful of smoke, "Why is that good?"

"No reason to be in such a hurry anymore. Give me one of those cigarettes."

Something in the sound of her voice struck a chord in my head, and suddenly I was very aware of the fact that I was standing in a darkened closet with a beautiful girl I knew absolutely nothing about. My stomach clenched and then unclenched, and I felt the beer moving up my gullet. With a grimace I forced it back down. Below my waist, I felt a sudden pressure and hoped that nobody yanked the door open before my problem subsided. And that Lucy didn't bump into me by mistake. Embarrassed, I backed away a step and felt the wall behind me. A coat hook dug into one of my shoulder blades.

Lucy lit another match and I handed her one of the cigarettes. She took a deep pull and closed her eyes, savoring it, then took a drink of beer, switching the match deftly from hand to hand as she maneuvered.

As the match started to flicker, she finished her second beer and dropped it on the ground. Just before we were plunged back into darkness, she looked me directly in the eyes.

"You seem like a nice guy, Paul," she said. The light went out.

For a moment I heard nothing, then someone laughed outside and voices chimed in. More laughter.

I felt her hands on my face, then down my neck, settling for the briefest moment on my chest. A strange sound escaped my mouth. *Wait*, I wanted to say. *This isn't me.*

The hands moved lower, over my stomach, and I knew she was kneeling because her fingers were pointed up. I could feel them digging playfully into my stomach.

There was a slight pressure as Lucy undid the button of my jeans, the sound of my zipper being drawn down. I turned my head toward the door, wanted to reach out and grab the doorknob. Someone could open the door at any moment. What if Steve thought we were taking too long and just....

I felt her pull me free and her hand was cool and smooth. I felt her breathe on me and then the lightest touch of her tongue, and then I was so hard it hurt and there was a pressure building in my stomach and in my head.

I wanted to warn her, tried to get the words out, but it was too late and my head went staticky as I turned inside-out, my hips bucking, the coat hook ramming so hard into my back I'd still have a bruise there a week later. I shuddered a last time and felt my sweat turn suddenly cold, as if my whole body had pins-and-needles.

"Oh, God," I whispered, and my voice was shaking. "I'm sorry." The words were humiliating to say; the only thing I was aware of was wanting to be somewhere else or dead or both.

She said nothing, just tucked me back into my pants, and I

zipped myself up, still shaking. She put her hands against my chest, leaned in close, and whispered. "Our secret, Paul. Just you and me." She lit a match and her eyes were dark and bright. "Our secret," she said. She opened her last beer and drank, and I did the same. When we both finished, we opened the closet door.

CHAPTER SIX

I still don't know what happened with the rest of the game, and I don't suppose it matters anymore. I never heard about any rule having been made, and other than Roscoe, no one seemed to notice my sudden departure. When Lucy and I emerged from the closet, I left the house and stumbled as far as the end of the long drive before I heard the first rumblings of thunder.

Instead of coming from any direction, the thunder seemed to come from all around me, vibrating in my arms and head and feet. Another clap of thunder ripped through the night, and almost immediately the world exploded into blue light, the lightning silhouetting trees and buildings and lampposts.

Suddenly there was a wind so powerful I couldn't find air to breathe. My mind went blank and I started running in no particular direction, looking for something to take shelter beneath. Around me the world flashed and bellowed, and each time it did, I covered my head with my arms, searching from beneath them for something I recognized. Old newspapers and leaves skittered by on the road and sidewalk, and I had to lean into the wind to avoid being knocked off balance.

And then, so quickly it seemed I'd simply neglected to notice earlier, rain was all around me, the kind of rain where the air

49

is suddenly solid water and there isn't enough air to breathe, and I couldn't see five feet in front of me. A gray shaped loomed up ahead and I stopped beneath the tree, resting my hands on the wet bark, shielded somewhat from the deluge by the tree's canopy. I looked around, saw that I was only feet from a cross-street, and strained to see the name on the sign.

But then the sign was gone, and so was everything else, and the concussion hit me so hard I fell down backwards onto the sidewalk and rapped my head hard on the concrete. I opened my eyes and saw a tree across the street explode into yellow and white flame and then collapse with a groan, and a ground-shaking thud into the lawn of the house it fronted, tearing down power and telephone lines as it went.

"Jesus," I said, pushing back to my feet, shaking and unsteady. The outline of the burning tree flamed on my corneas each time I blinked, and my head felt like it was stuffed full of wet towels, all of the sounds around me muffled and indistinct.

As I waited beneath the tree, my eyes gradually cleared and I realized that the rain had dissipated somewhat. The street sign was visible and I could see the word DOYLE, and knew where I was. Some of the panic went out of my chest and I left the shelter of the tree and ran toward Smith, hunched against a wind that had suddenly turned bitter-cold.

And then I was back in the room, fumbling at my jeans with shivering fingers, shucking off wet clothing onto the floor. It was all I could do to pull a blanket out of the closet before I fell face down on the bed, grasping the blanket tightly about me. My stomach was doing flips and the taste of beer foamed on the back of my tongue.

I slept for twelve hours, and when I finally woke up at noon the next day, I'd missed both of my morning classes. I had one more, at three o'clock, but instead of getting dressed I climbed back into bed. Something was wrong; I didn't know what exactly, but inside of me, somewhere in my chest or in my head, something wasn't working correctly. Over and over I told myself that I was going to get up now, that I was going to take a shower and then read or write or get something to eat, but I never did.

Every time I thought about climbing out of bed I would remember what had happened with Lucy in the closet, and then I would see the tree exploding in a flash of metallic silver-white and my body would flood with shame and fear and bright panic.

I thought about Jo at college and imagined talking to her on the phone, and was suddenly certain that at this very moment she was asleep naked in bed with some burly fraternity guy, the sheets twisted around her legs, his semen dried to a taut crust on her thighs, streaks of saliva shiny across her stomach and breasts. Something malignant was building inside of me, *massing* there. I could feel my throat distend with it and tried to swallow, but found it wouldn't move.

I opened my mouth to say something to the empty room, or to try to get the lump out of my air pipe, but all that came out was a low moan. Then I was up suddenly and moving, pacing from my bed to the bathroom door and back again, over and over. My hands were sweating and I twisted the fabric of my T-shirt in my fingers, trying to dry them. An electric buzzing filled my head; I felt it vibrating in my scalp and in the backs of my eyes, which had begun to water. I wanted desperately to stop moving, to pull back from the black hole that suddenly yawned beneath my feet, but it consumed me, pulling me down and down. How I had gotten to this point I had no idea, but I was afraid. In the truest and deepest part of me, I believed I was going to die.

I was lying in bed, curled up on my side underneath the blanket, when Roscoe came back to the room sometime after dark. By this time the sobs had tailed off, but my eyes were still teary. Roscoe closed the door and stood just inside the room, looking at me.

"Paco," he said, "you okay?"

"Fine," I said, and would have asked him to please leave me alone if I'd trusted my voice.

He nodded and looked at the floor. I rolled onto my back and stared at the linked-wire bottom of the top bunk. After a moment I heard the sound of Roscoe's feet and then the door. I exhaled, wanting only to be alone again. Then he was back, carrying a folding chair. He set it down next to the bed, plopped into it, then put his feet up on the edge of my mattress.

"So what's the deal, man?" he said, folding his hands over his stomach and leaning back in the chair.

I shook my head and fixed my gaze on the top bunk again. There was silence and I could hear people yelling somewhere down the hall, then laughing. For a moment I wanted to tell Roscoe about what had happened with Lucy, and about the tree, but I couldn't do it.

"Have you been up at all today?" Roscoe said. When I didn't answer, he shook the bed with his foot. "Hey, come on, Paco."

"What do you want from me?" I snapped. "I feel like shit. Can't you just leave me alone?"

"That what you want?"

"Yes," I said, looking over at him.

He smiled at me and shook his head. "No, it's not," he said, then added, "Hey, open that window, wouldya?" He pointed past me at the window next to the bunk as he pulled out his cigarettes and a pack of matches.

Exasperated, I sat up and unlocked the window, then pushed it up. I'd become so accustomed to the heat that the slap of cool air which blew into the room shocked me, but it felt good. Rising from the dining hall downstairs I could smell ground beef and onions and fried potatoes, and my stomach churned hungrily.

I heard the sound of a match being struck and turned back to Roscoe, who was lighting his smoke. He held the pack out to

52

me, and after a moment I took one and leaned forward to light it off of Roscoe's match. I shimmied back and propped myself up against the metal frame of the bed and pulled lightly on the cigarette, not really liking the taste, but not hating it either.

"Wait a sec," Roscoe said, standing. "You know what we need?" He didn't finish the thought, but went to his closet and fumbled around in the jumble of clothing and shoes and other assorted crap on the floor. When he straightened, he had a bottle in his hand. "Aha," he said, then sat back down in his chair.

"What's that?" I asked, eyeing the bottle skeptically. The label was white and said Canada Club.

"Honestly," Roscoe said, "it's really skanked-out cheap whiskey. I won't lie to you because you feel bad already, and I don't want to set you up for disappointment."

I grunted. "Thanks."

Roscoe twisted the cap off the bottle and handed it to me. "Give it a try?"

My first instinct was to say no, but I realized that I *did* want to try it. I raised the bottle and sniffed, got an eye-watering nose-full of alcohol fumes, and recoiled.

"Go ahead," Roscoe said. "It tastes better than it smells. Not much, but a little."

And he was right. I'd expected it to taste like gasoline, but it wasn't so awful, and when it moved down my throat and into my stomach, it lit everything it touched with a fiery burn. I handed the bottle to Roscoe. He took a swig, eyes closed, and let out a contented "Mmm" as he lowered the bottle from his lips. He handed the bottle back to me and I drank again, more this time, liking very much the way the whiskey felt going down. When I took a drag from my cigarette, even it tasted better.

"Look," Roscoe said, his eyes closed. "I don't think you want to talk about whatever's going on with you right now, but if you do, I'm game." He opened his eyes and looked at me. "For what it's worth, I think you're homesick. Maybe that's wrong, but I don't think so."

Instead of saying anything, I stared straight ahead, feeling a combination of shame and outrage. What was I, a six year-old? Homesick? It was insulting to hear someone my own age accuse me of something I associated with children. I wanted to tell him to keep his stupid theories to himself.

But the more I thought about it, especially the next day and in the days after that, I realized how accurate Roscoe's diagnosis probably was. Homesick for my house and parents? To a certain extent that was true; I loved my mother and father and missed them. But more to the point, I was homesick for who I'd been. I missed the sense of simplicity and clarity I used to feel. Now everything felt complicated and wrong, and I just wanted it to feel okay again.

Roscoe took another drink, then said, "You hungry?"

Realizing that he was just as eager to change the subject as I was, I said, "Yeah. I can't remember the last thing I ate."

"Then let's go downstairs. I could eat the asshole out of a wooden Indian."

***

Nothing was the same after that. I went out with Roscoe almost every night, most frequently to the Hill, where we made runs at every fraternity house, sopping their beer up like sponges. Our most consistent haunt was Sigma Theta, where we usually spent our time in Steve's room, drinking with Steve, Jerome, and Dan. Sometimes the girls would be there, too, but more often it was just us, sitting around, getting drunk, and playing beer pong or three-man or just talking. And when we'd gotten drunk, we'd move on to some other house, some other party.

In those first few weeks Roscoe and I sat on sagging couches and broken easy chairs in hundreds of rooms, sucking from cans and bottles of Pabst Blue Ribbon, Natural Pilsner, and Miller beer. When there were cigarettes, I smoked them, and soon I was making trips once or twice a week to the United Dairy Farmers mini-mart across the road from Smith Hall, buying my own packs of Camels.

Sometimes in the morning I'd wake up and roll over, sweaty and clammy and hung-over, look at the bottom of Roscoe's bunk, and wonder what I was doing. Who I was. I'd get up and catch up on as much of my reading as I could in a day, fighting a newly-developing inability to concentrate on anything for more than ten minutes, and then, in the evening, Roscoe would stick his head into the study room and say, "Hey, Paco, get your shit together. We're going out." And off we'd go.

I knew that what I was doing was stupid, that I was hurting myself. But I handled it, and sometimes even liked who I was becoming when I looked at myself from the outside. I let my facial hair grow in for the first time in my life. My body turned the beer into flesh and my frame filled out. I stopped tucking in my shirts and wore whatever was clean. In a way, it felt like I was letting myself go, but I knew it was more than that, and I looked at what I was doing with a brand of objective fascination.

My grades, though undoubtedly lower than my parents would like when they saw my grade-report, held steady at B in most courses. The only class where my grade was suffering dramatically was Fiction Workshop. I knew I had to get my ass in gear and actually write something, but each time I tried, Roscoe would appear in the doorway and announce our imminent departure for some fraternity party.

From time to time I would see Lucy up at Sigma Theta, sometimes in Steve's room, sometimes hanging out in the third floor hallway where there was always a game of beer pong or quarters or poker taking place. When she saw me she would smile and say hello, and I would bumble something out, then find a place where I could look at her without being seen. I saw

55

the way she received and rejected the guys who came on to her, saw the way she was virtually ignored by all but a few of the girls who hung out at the house. She was a strange presence there, out of place but constant.

Then, on Halloween, Delt threw a costume party at one of their off-campus houses. Roscoe and I tossed on the simplest outfits we could scrounge up — black pants and shirts and night-watchmen caps — and called ourselves cat burglars.

As soon as we arrived, Roscoe locked onto a girl dressed as Smurfette and headed off in her direction, swearing that he had — just *had* — to see what she looked like under all that blue body paint, and I went in search of the keg, which someone told me was in the yard in the back of the house. As soon as I rounded the corner, I saw Lucy.

Although the temperature at night must have been somewhere in the mid-forties, she was dressed like Barbara Eden from *I Dream of Jeanie*. She wore sparkling sequined bottoms and a sheer pink top, with a pink wrap around her hair. Her stomach was bare and I stared at it, at the gentle bumps of her hip bones, the slight concavity of her belly. I made up my mind to say something, anything, but then there was a guy dressed as Dracula carrying two beers next to her. And then there was Steve, decked out as a cowboy, gun belts crisscrossed on his hips.

I was too far away to hear Steve's words, but I could read the expression on his face perfectly. Anger. His eyes were too wide and his forehead and neck burned red, and he pushed closer to Dracula until they stood nose to nose. Dracula drew back, hands upheld, and Steve turned to say something to Lucy, but she had walked away.

CHAPTER SEVEN

By the time November tenth rolled around, the heat that had marked the beginning of school was a distant, almost surreal memory. The air turned dry and cold. Sometimes I would wake up in the morning and step outside Smith, and the arid air would score my lungs like thousands of tiny diamonds. Often the breeze would bring the smell of a wood fire burning, and even as a grown man, when I smelled that odor I would be eighteen again, stepping outside the front door of Smith Hall. It was the smell of being alive and content and full of potential.

The leaves on the trees had changed and then started to fall off; sitting outside, you could hear the rasp of dried leaves skittering across concrete. Sometimes after class, when I wasn't ready to deal with the work I knew I should be doing, I would come back to the dorm and sit on the low wall surrounding the patio outside the dining hall, reading and smoking, or just watching people walk by on the paved path leading to the academic side of campus.

Just as the late summer storm had ended the heat wave, my meltdown after the party at the old mansion had ushered in better weather as well; I felt alive and good, like myself, but a new, *better* myself.

57

The cold snap switched something on inside of me. In the two weeks before mid-semester break, I'd churned out three stories, two of which were passable, one of which I thought might be legitimately good. My prof in the Fiction Writing class, Isaac O'Connor, had verified my hunch. He'd given me the names of a few mid-level literary magazines, and I'd sent the story off.

Because I'd been spending more time writing, my nightly trips with Roscoe to the Hill slowed. When I went out, it was on a Friday or Saturday night, and I never got so drunk that the next day would be a completely hung-over waste.

I could actually remember the moment my life had leveled out, or at least the moment I *realized* that it had. As with many of the most important passages in my life, it was totally pedestrian; I was going through the dinner line in the Smith dining hall, scooping a slab of meatloaf, then some corn, then some green beans onto my tri-sectioned plastic plate, when I suddenly realized that I was happy. Roscoe wasn't there, nor was Steve. And I wasn't thinking about Lucy. I was simply content, happy to be where I was. For the first time in my life, I was truly comfortable in my own skin. When a girl behind me in line asked if I was all right, I realized that I'd probably been standing in front of the veggies for a while. I told her yes and thank you, then found a place to sit.

When I'd arrived at Penton two months before, I was naïve, sheltered. Understandably, I'd gone a little nuts for a while. That was fine — the damage was minimal — and now, thankfully, I'd managed to find some kind of balance in my life.

Which wasn't to say that things were perfect.

Lucy still haunted my thoughts. On several occasions since our encounter in the closet, I had spasmed awake with the feel of her hand on me, soft and warm and gently pulling. It had occurred to me more than once that, although I spent much of those first two months at school drunk or stoned or both, I had never so much as kissed another girl. There had been opportunities, certainly.

On one particularly memorable occasion, a girl I walked home from an off-campus party closed her dorm room door behind us, pulled a condom from under her mattress, and said, "This is how I say thank you."

Three other girls had propositioned me overtly at Sigma Theta, and dozens of others had been so drunk that they'd likely have gone home with a gorilla — Roscoe's conquests were proof of that — but for whatever reason, none of them had truly interested me.

In the way of rationalization, I told myself that I turned them down because I wasn't ready to have sex, because going home with any of them would have jeopardized my ability to look at myself as a decent guy. But that was crap.

The truth of the matter was that I didn't care about the girls because they weren't Lucy. I could look at other girls and find them attractive, but I wanted nothing to do with them. In that way, Lucy was all I could think of, but even though I found myself looking for her everywhere I went, I almost never saw her for more than a passing moment. And I had to admit that sometimes it almost seemed better that way. What if she came straight up to me and started talking? What the hell would I say? It was the difference between seeing a lion through the bars and being in the cage.

I was going to see her. There was nothing I could do about that, and even if there was, I wouldn't have wanted my occasional encounters with her to stop. But neither could I argue that my belly didn't clench each time I passed Lucy in the hall at Sig Theta, or when I saw her ahead of me on the Jaywalk when I was on my way to class. That's just the way it was.

Until the night before mid-semester break.

***

Roscoe came into the study room on our floor and found me in the over-stuffed chair by the window, smoking and trying to force myself through a chapter in my art history book on the Little Dutch Masters. Though I loved the artwork itself, there was only so much I could stand to know about the personal lives of Honthorst and Van Eyck.

"Paco," he said, sitting down in the chair across from mine, "you coming tonight?"

Earlier he'd mentioned a party up at Sigma Theta and I'd told him I'd think about it. He was headed back to Pennsylvania in the morning for break, but since my parents were going to be in Florida visiting my mother's sister, I was staying put, which was fine with me. The idea for a new story had popped into my head, and I was looking forward to seeing where it went. Unlike much of what I'd written to that point, the idea was for a horror story, and I wanted to see what it would feel like to actually put those words on the page. I had always enjoyed reading the suspense and horror novels my mom would read and then discard around the house in whatever bookshelf happened to be nearby, and I felt no shame for sharing in her Peter Straub and Stephen King addictions. Reading those stories was one thing, but to actually *write* those words down? Something about it felt taboo, and I couldn't deny the excitement I felt.

"I don't think so, man," I said. "I feel like something a little more low-key tonight. Thought I might walk into town and see a show at The Strand." The Strand was Penton's only movie theater. It was small and privately owned and, best of all, it was almost always empty. Since this was a weekday, I knew tonight would be no exception. I'd see an early show, something nasty hopefully, then come home and crank on the story until I couldn't keep my eyes open anymore.

Roscoe looked at me quietly, and I knew that he was irritated. After a month of going out with him almost every night, I'd pulled back. I felt guilty about it, but I was better off this way. Finally, a look of grudging acceptance came into his eyes.

60

"Okay," he said, "but at least come back to the room and drink a beer with me."

"Sure," I said.

***

Later that night, after Roscoe had taken off for the Hill, I got dressed in jeans and a heavy sweater, then pulled on my black pea coat and my watchman's cap and headed out.

The night was cool, but bearable. As I walked toward town, I lit a Camel and alternated hands while I smoked it, keeping the one I wasn't using stuffed in a pocket of my coat. I felt good. Almost unnaturally good, like I was floating. Maybe it was the idea of writing that raised my mood. Maybe it was the fact that I was finally balancing my life in the way I'd always hoped I would. Or maybe, in retrospect, it was because in some rarely-used part of my brain, I knew I'd see Lucy. I'd never been one to believe in ESP or prognostication or any of the other supernormal mumbo-jumbo of the mind, but even now, I can remember the way I felt that night, energized and confident.

Passing through Penton, I said hello to a few students I knew as they wandered toward the Backstretch or The West End. Where Penton in that nearly insufferable dog-day summer had been a ghost town, it was bustling with life in this early-winter season. White Christmas lights hung in the row of young oak trees that lined the side of Sandusky Street, and for the first time I thought of going home for Thanksgiving in just a couple of weeks, and then again for Christmas in a little over a month. The thought saddened me, and I almost laughed aloud at that. Just weeks ago I had walked through town with Roscoe, nearly crying from my homesick depression, and now I could barely stand the thought of leaving.

As I approached The Strand, I read the lighted marquee above the double-doors. Triumph. One of the two movies playing was *Back to the Future*, which I'd seen already, but some twisted soul

61

had also decided to break out their old reel of *The Exorcist*. I'd seen the movie when it came out a couple of years before, but I'd been in the mood for something nasty. I purchased a ticket at the box office for the 8:30 show and went inside.

There were two people other than me standing inside the concession area. One was a bored-looking girl in a red uniform behind the concession stand. She was in my Fiction Writing workshop, and though she never seemed to recognize me, she was unmistakable with her horrible acne and sullen, perpetually frowning mouth. She wrote stories about incest so hackneyed and detailed I thought they were probably a form of fantasy, not a reflection of her own experiences. Each time I'd come to The Strand, she'd been working. Currently, she was reading a copy of T.S. Eliot's *The Wasteland* and chewing on a soft pretzel.

The other person was a middle-aged man with Coke-bottle glasses and a matching case of acne. He stood leaning on the glass case that housed the candy, and wore a bright blue shirt with the words WHERE WE'RE GOING WE DON'T NEED ROADS stenciled across the front.

I asked the girl for a small popcorn and a Coke, then walked down a hallway to my theater.

The Strand was as old-fashioned as it got. The ridiculously small movie screen—which in my memory was no more than eight feet square, but may have been smaller—was framed on both sides by crimson curtains, and the walls themselves were lined with light-absorbing black fabric. The seats were upholstered in black as well, and they were so plush that when you sat down, they seemed to swallow you up completely. I chose a seat in the middle of the tiny theater, shucked off my coat, and deposited it on the chair next to me.

As I waited for the movie to start, I pulled a notepad from my coat pocket and flipped through the notes I'd taken for the new story. The idea had come to me a week or so ago while I was sitting on the couch in Steve's room, watching TV and having a few beers. Steve had the TV tuned in to PBS—I couldn't count the episodes of *NOVA* I'd seen since I started hanging out with him—and the current show was about the treatment of livestock on American farms. Completely unbidden, it occurred to me to wonder what it would be like to run a farm where human beings were the livestock. When I went home that night, I hesitated in front of my desk for an indecisive moment, then scribbled the idea down on a piece of typing paper and tucked it beneath a corner of my IBM Selectric.

Now, days later, I had a rough outline of the plot progression. The events and images were so violent and bizarre, it was hard to imagine myself actually sitting down and typing the words. And showing it to other people when I was done? The thought made me laugh to myself.

"What's so funny?"

I jerked like I'd been cattle-prodded and dropped the pad, and heard my pen rolling away under the seats. Looking up, my heart a pulsing fist in my throat, I saw Lucy.

"Jesus," I said.

"Nope. I don't think he'd be seen dead at this movie." Lucy moved my coat into the next seat and sat down beside me, then set her drink on the floor. "Sorry I scared you. What were you working on?"

The notepad.

I bent down and picked it up, thought for a second about looking for the pen, then pictured myself on all fours searching for it, ass in the air. I decided that there were other pens in the world.

"Nothing," I said. "Just an idea I had for a story." I felt hot and my throat still throbbed with my pulse. I forced myself to smile and look at Lucy.

"You write? What kind of stuff?"

"Uhm, usually I end up writing the same kinds of stories over and over. Mothers, fathers, kids."

"What's this one about?"

I blushed. Just telling her about the story would be humiliating. She'd think I was a freak and a pervert. "I don't think you want to know."

"You can't say something like that and then *not* tell me. That'd be cruel. Now I *know* it's got to be good." She'd turned in her seat so that she faced me, one leg pulled up and tucked under her. As I looked at her, I realized how slender and delicate she really was. It wasn't merely a matter of her waifish size; it was also the way her face and body were put together, slightly off-center, not quite cohesive, as if she might fall to pieces at any moment.

"Well, I don't want to be cruel," I said back to her, then sat thinking of how to explain the story.

"Look," she said, resting one of her hands softly on my knee. "Just start at the beginning." She looked both ways as if to make sure we were still alone in the theater, then leaned towards me, a smile pulling at the corners of her mouth. "You can tell me anything."

My face went hot instantly, and before I knew it I was babbling, telling her all about the story, why I was afraid to write it, that I feared my parents seeing a copy of it and wondering where they went so wrong in raising me, and about half-a-dozen other things that had nothing to do with anything. In short, anything to avoid a silence where she might say something else that would make me feel crazy.

"You feel weird about writing it," she said when I finished. "Why?"

I shrugged. "You write stuff about a kid who's pissed at his dad and people say, 'Aw, cute.' You write something like this...."

"Fuck what other people think. Do what you want."

Finally, the lights in the theater dimmed and the projector

64

flickered into life. I turned to face the screen and propped my feet up on the seat in front of me.

As the opening scene of *The Exorcist* whirred into life, Lucy leaned in close and brushed her lips softly against my cheek. My stomach did a sickening little flip.

"Remember what happened last time we were in a dark room together?" she whispered, then leaned back in her seat to watch the movie.

***

I spent most of the time in the movie sneaking what I hoped were subtle looks over at Lucy, who seemed to be completely engrossed. Between my sideways glances, I found myself caught up in what was happening to poor Reagan McNeal, the little girl possessed by a demon determined to kill her. For a little while I lost myself the way I always had as a kid.

Then, about an hour and a half into the movie, I glanced over at Lucy and saw that she had fallen asleep. Her head rested against the back of the seat and was tilted against one of her shoulders. I thought for a moment about waking her up, but didn't. At quiet points in the movie I could hear the soft sound of her breathing. When the movie ended she opened her eyes as if she'd set some kind of mental alarm clock.

"Sorry," she said, yawning, "I've seen that one before. I love scary movies, but once you've seen 'em...." She stood and pulled her sweater on. "Are you going to walk me home?" she asked, taking a pair of powder-blue gloves from her pocket and tugging them on.

"Uh, yeah, sure," I said, shrugging into my own coat.

"Good."

Chapter Eight

When we stepped out of The Strand it was a little after ten o'clock. The temperature had dropped significantly, and our breath puffed out in front of us as Lucy and I headed back toward campus.

In my heavy sweater and pea coat I was warm, but Lucy hadn't dressed for the weather, and a couple of minutes into our walk I could see her start to shiver beneath the thin, cream-colored cardigan she wore.

"Do you want my coat?" I asked as we waited for the traffic light at Spring and Sandusky.

The look on Lucy's face as she turned to answer my question was my first true introduction to her. The girl I'd been with in the closet was only a tiny part of her personality, one brick in a massive structure. The real Lucy was nearly fluid in her range of emotion; as time went by and I came to know her better, I'd realize that her mercurial nature had its roots deep in her past, but at that moment, standing on the corner and waiting for the light to change, I was transfixed by what I saw.

Hard eyes, steely and unforgiving, then softening, warming at the corners, somehow shrewdly calculating and measuring at the same time. Finally, settling somewhere between all of the above.

"You don't mind?" she said. "It's cold."

"My sweater'll keep me just fine." I shucked off the black pea coat and held it for Lucy while she slipped her arms into the sleeves. She buttoned it and then stepped back, raising her arms theatrically and striking a pose.

"So, what do you think?"

I couldn't help but laugh. I wasn't a giant by any stretch of the imagination, but my coat may as well have belonged to one, the way it billowed around her slight frame. The bottom hem fell halfway between her hips and her knees, and the wide sleeves outreached her fingertips by inches.

Looking at her brought to mind a picture in one of the family albums at home: me as a kid, wearing my dad's black college graduation robe, cum laude sash, and mortarboard, draped in billowing black fabric. That's how Lucy looked now, like a kid wearing her dad's clothes.

"It works for you," I said. "Tres chic." At that moment the light turned green. As we crossed Sandusky Street, Lucy slipped her arm through mine and leaned into me.

"What do you feel like doing now?" she said as we stepped up onto the opposite curb. The question caught me a little off-guard since I'd been operating under the assumption that I was walking her back to her dorm, not that I had any idea what dorm she lived in.

"Dunno," I said. "Only thing I ever really do down here is go to the movies. What else is there?"

She thought for a moment, looking down Sandusky one way and then the other. After a moment, a slow smile made its way across her face.

"I know," she said, reaching down and taking my hand. "Come on." I followed her lead, very aware of her hand inside my own, wondering what it meant. My nerve endings were working overtime; every time I took a step, her hand shifted in mine and I felt a rush of her presence. *She took my hand,* I thought. *What the hell is up with that?*

"Can I ask you something?" Lucy said. We had passed through town and were heading in the general direction of Smith and the rest of the dorms.

"Sure."

"Where did that scar come from? The one on your forearm. I saw it in the theater. It must have been painful."

Whatever I'd expected her to ask, it wasn't that. I hitched the sleeve of my sweater and held my arm up, looking down at the pale scar on the inside of my forearm. Its center was about the size of a half-dollar, and the surrounding skin was crisscrossed by seven or eight slender tentacles of scar tissue. There were a few additional splotches on my bicep and stomach, another on my wrist, but my forearm had gotten the worst of it. I remembered my last night in Swarthmore, lying with Jo on the couch, the feel of her fingers on my arm, the thought I'd had that she knew everything about me. Suddenly I realized that wasn't true anymore. Things had changed. *I* had changed.

"It's not a fun story," I said. "I don't know if you really want to hear it."

"Try me," she said.

"Okay," I said, figuring there was no graceful way out. "What the hell." I took a deep breath. "When I was eight my mom was in the kitchen frying chicken in a skillet on the stove. I'd been out playing with my friends all day, and they were all going over to someone's house for a sleepover and I wanted to go, too. So I went up to my mom to ask her and tugged on her shirt, and she turned to look at me." I took a steadying breath and then blew it out slowly.

"You okay?" Lucy said.

"Yeah, this is just one of those memories, you know?"

She nodded. "You can stop if you want. I didn't want to make you feel bad."

"That's okay," I said. "I'm already halfway there." I took a deep breath. "So she turns to look at me and at the same time the cat, Julie, who had been sitting on the windowsill above the sink, jumps down and knocks her arm."

"Oh, Jesus," Lucy said. "You're kidding me."

I shook my head. "So the oil goes flying everywhere and I fall down backwards and hit my head on one of the stools at the breakfast bar. I could feel the oil on my arm and I could hear...I could hear this sizzling sound, but then I blacked out, just fainted, you know."

Lucy had taken a cigarette out of her pocket and paused for a second to light it. Ahead, I could see the lights of Smith and Stuyvesant and Welch. "Did the oil get you anywhere else?" she asked. There wasn't a trace of discomfort in her voice, just level curiosity.

"On my stomach a little," I said. "But I didn't get the worst of it."

"Your mom?" Lucy winced.

I shook my head again. "When I came to, I didn't even feel the burn on my arm at first. All I remember was hearing this awful sound and the smell of something burning. I thought it was me. I mean, my arm felt *atomic*. My mom was kneeling next to me, screaming for my dad to come. I'd fallen almost underneath the breakfast bar, and when I turned to look for whatever was making the sound, I saw the cat. She was lying on the ground, just twitching. Oil had gotten all over one side of her head, and there was no hair left there anymore. Her mouth just opened and closed, and there was this noise like she was screaming underwater. Then I blacked out again, and when I woke up I was in the ER with my parents."

"Did you ask about the cat?"

"No. I knew it was dead. Can I have some of that?" I asked, and Lucy handed me her smoke. I took a drag and handed it back. "So, how's that for an uncomfortable story?"

"Not bad," she said. "But I'm not uncomfortable."

I laughed. "Guess I'll just have to try harder."

"Do your worst."

***

Before we reached our final destination for the night, Lucy and I made two stops. The first was at the United Dairy Farmer's store across from my dorm, where Lucy bought a twelve-pack of Pabst Blue Ribbon beer.

"Where to now?" I asked, taking the beer from her.

"Food," Lucy said. "Something tasty."

"Tasty," I repeated.

"Yup. Something nice and greasy." She clapped her hands. "Got it. Let's go." And we were off again, this time to Tim's Pizza, the only pizza joint in town. Lucy and I waited outside and smoked for the ten minutes it took for Tim, or whoever was slaving away in the kitchen that night, to prepare our order. I paid for the pie and followed Lucy back outside into the cold.

"You're being a real sport about this," she said, lighting a cigarette and handing it to me, then lighting one for herself.

I took a drag and nodded. "Yeah, I'm a real sport. I *am* wondering where the hell we're taking this feast, though."

She smiled. "Then let's satisfy your curiosity, shall we?"

Five minutes later we were on the academic side of campus, which was all but deserted at this time of night. Because so many of the students had already taken off for mid-semester break, there were even fewer out than normal. Finally, Lucy stopped in front of Sturges Hall, the building that housed the English and Humanities departments, and turned to me.

"Well," she said. "What do you think?"

"I think it's the English building," I said.

"Wow. Impressive grasp of the obvious, Paul." Her words were dry, but the look on her face was one of barely restrained excitement.

I waited for her to clue me in to whatever plan she'd fomented in her head, but when she didn't I said, "So...the English building."

She nodded. "We're breaking in. You go around that way." She pointed to the dark alleyway between Sturges and Slocum Hall. "Sometimes the profs forget to close the windows."

Still fighting to comprehend what she'd just said to me, and the matter-of-fact way she'd said it, I blurted out, "But the cleaning crew—"

"The cleaning people fucking *hate* most of the profs, Paul. The woman who does the first floor of Sturges, Esmerelda, told me that if she had to close one more window because some hoity-toity English fag—her words—was too lazy to do it himself, she was going to go ahead and leave it open and let the cards fall where they may."

Hip-high shrubs bordered the building, and Lucy quickly stooped and stashed the pizza box behind one, then took the beer from my hands and secreted it away as well. When she looked back up, she must have seen something in my expression—Lucy could read people like nobody I've ever known—because she chuckled and said, "What? Does it shock you to know that I talk to the cleaning crew?"

"No," I said, though that wasn't true. The truth was that I was having an *extremely* difficult time picturing Lucy in a conversation with one of the blue-clad women, most of whom were black, who cleaned the dorms and academic buildings in which we spent our days and nights. Not for the first time, and certainly not for the last, I remembered how little I really knew about this girl.

"They're nice people," she said. "And they like *us* a hell of a lot more than they like the faculty. It's amazing what kind of information a cup of coffee can buy you. Now go."

Moving as inconspicuously as possible, I skirted the outside of the big old building. I passed by the classroom where I sat from one until two every Monday, Wednesday, and Friday for my Freshman Comp class, and then two other shut windows. The next window I came to, however, was slightly cracked, just enough so that, if the professor left the door of the classroom open, a crisp draft would flow in to temper the often-sweltering heat tossed off by the overenthusiastic boiler.

Something tightened in my brain. I looked both ways, feeling suddenly guilty and very exposed, though I'd not yet done anything wrong. The campus was empty in all directions, dark save for the pools of light cast by the evenly spaced arc sodium lamps. All the tests had been taken, the papers turned in. Most the remaining students were probably holed-up in their rooms drinking or smoking grass, or downtown at the Backstretch.

Close it, a voice in my head whispered to me urgently. *Close the window and tell Lucy that you didn't see anything.*

But I knew I wouldn't do that. Looking back now, I recognize that night as one where, had I only *listened* to the just-emerging man inside of me, I could have avoided all of the awfulness that was to come. When you're eighteen, however, and in the company of a beautiful girl, you hear that voice, that almost-grown-up presence in your head, as the expression of childish fear and anxiety, not wisdom. So I did what I couldn't help but do; I waited for Lucy to come around the corner of the building, and when she did, I ran back for the pizza and the beer.

CHAPTER NINE

I pushed up the window, wincing at the dry, throaty rasp of painted wood against painted wood. Making a stirrup with my hands, I boosted Lucy up onto the four-foot high sill, handed her our supplies, then hoisted myself up and into the dark classroom. I closed the window and pulled the vinyl shade down, heart pumping somewhere between my chest and throat.

"Relax," Lucy said, and handed me the beer. "Esmerelda says she's always done here by eight, nine at the latest, and that nobody ever comes in until the next day." She locked me with her gaze and grinned. "Good find, by the way."

"What?" I said.

"The window. I wasn't sure you'd tell me even if you *did* find one that was open. I thought that maybe you'd just close it and say 'Sorry, Luce, shit luck. What's plan B?'"

I had a realization then, the kind of epiphany you don't need to have corroborated, but which you can speak aloud with absolute certainty.

"You knew that window was open," I said. "You knew because you were the one who opened it. You had me go around the building the way I did because you wanted to see if I'd tell you when I found it." A new feeling had seeped into my head, one I wasn't prepared for. I felt angry. This entire night—hell, since the moment she'd *met* me—Lucy had been playing me, leading me on. It was emasculating, and I shook my head slowly and took a deep breath, trying to expel the sour feeling in my chest.

"Not bad, Paul," she said, and there was something that might have been respect in her eyes and in her voice. "I have Public Life and Private Lives in this room. The professor who teaches it, Langden, usually takes off right away at the end of class, so today I just waited for the room to clear out, and then...."

"So you knew you'd be back here tonight?"

"Yeah," she said. "Going to the movie was just to get some thinking done, but I knew I'd be here later, one way or another. But I didn't know I'd be here with you. Come on."

I followed her into the hallway, past framed prints of blown-up book covers—*Pride and Prejudice, Bleak House, Leaves of Grass*—bulletin boards crammed with overlapping layers of fliers, announcements, ads for coffee house poetry readings, concerts, parties, articles cut out of newspapers about the hole in the ozone layer, about Reagan's election to a second term, the arms race. This was one of my favorite things about the English department at Penton; the professors and students were all over the place in terms of their politics and ideals.

More than anything else, it was strange to be in the familiar place at such an unfamiliar time. I felt like I had taken a step over an important moral boundary. I wasn't the guy who broke into academic buildings after hours; I was the guy who told his friends how stupid it would be to break into academic buildings after hours. Some of my anger dissipated and was replaced by the shaky feeling of fear I knew so well from my normal life. I shrugged my shoulders against a sudden shiver and moved a little faster to catch up with Lucy.

We climbed to the second floor, which housed the offices of the Humanities department.

"Wait here a sec," Lucy said, and handed me the pizza box. A moment later she was back with a ring of keys, which she twirled on her finger. "Onward and upward," she said.

I said, "Where'd you get those?" I'd assumed that breaking into the building and eating some food would be the extent of our criminal activity for the night, but now it looked like Lucy had something more in mind.

"Secretary's desk drawer," she answered. We reached the third floor, and headed in the direction of the faculty offices. "It's funny," Lucy continued. "They lock their doors, but the secretary doesn't even *have* a door, nor does she lock the drawer she keeps the master key in. Now does that make sense?"

She stopped in front of an office and I looked at the wooden name plaque. PROFESSOR COKER, PhD. And below that, in smaller letters, ENGLISH DEPT. To the little bulletin board on the door was tacked a schedule of office hours, a Dick Tracy comic strip, and a thin sheaf of papers. The title at the top of the first page was TIC-TAC-POE: EDGAR ALLEN POE'S INTELLECTUAL GAMESMANSHIP. Beneath that was the byline: Dr. Charles Coker, PhD.

Lucy was looking at the paper also. "No talent fuckwad probably couldn't get it published, so he decided to inflict it on the ranks of the obligated." The raw anger in her voice surprised me. To this point her demeanor had been almost carefree, and I'd been able to see all of this as some innocent prank. Now my tension jacked up another notch; there was more going on than I understood.

"Old professor?" I asked.

Lucy found the key she wanted, stuck it in the lock, and twisted. *Click.* She opened the door and turned to me.

"Freshman Comp," she said. "Ol' Chuck the Fuck, Piled High and Deep, decided to get himself a little coed play. Guess who the lucky girl was?" She stepped into the office and, after a moment of indecision, I followed. My nerves screamed as she closed the door behind us.

The same sentence that I knew from the few times I'd flown and from any other number of occasions where I was about to do something I probably shouldn't have been doing had started to run through my head: *This is a really bad idea this is a really bad idea this is a really bad idea....* But there I was, bad idea or not, and Lucy was talking.

"Yeah," she said, "Chuck and I have quite the history." Lucy was looking around the office, and for a moment I knew she wasn't entirely with me, but in the past. She reached out and plucked a framed photograph off Coker's desk. Even in the dim light I could see that it showed a bearded, dark-haired man with a woman, a youthful-looking blonde, and two young children.

She took a deep breath and I could see that her hands were trembling. Before I could even detect the movement, the framed photo of Coker and his family exploded against the wall. I rocked forward onto the balls of my feet and had to stop myself from stooping to pick the frame up, my first instinct.

"I told the bastard I would go to the administration, tell them he was grading me down because I wouldn't fuck him. But he just looked at me and said 'Don't you know, silly little Lucy, that dozens of complaints are brought against every male faculty member every year, and that the administration is used to hearing the made-up stories of confused little girls?'"

"Lucy, that can't be —"

"I know, I know," she said. "But at the time it...it made sense to me. I'd come to expect certain things from men, and it made sense. Jesus. I wanted to grab the letter opener off his desk and put it in his eye, but it made sense."

Lucy still shook, not just her hands, but her whole body, strong waves of rage rolling through her slight body with such power I almost expected her to fly apart. There was a leather blotter on the desk, and now, moving with a jerky fury, Lucy picked it up and twisted it, crumpled it, and then, realizing that she wouldn't be able to rip it apart, dropped it on the floor and stomped on it. Her beautiful face was contorted and red, and her saucer-wide eyes scared me.

She grabbed her hair with both hands and yanked, *hard*, and I could actually hear strands ripping out of her scalp, a sound I'll never forget. A guttural sound of anger and frustration came from somewhere deep inside of her, and when she dropped her hands from her head, I could see long hairs hanging from her fingers.

Before I could stop myself, I took a step toward her, my hands outstretched, but she stepped back and said, "Don't."

"Lucy," I said, hearing the frightened shake in my voice. "No matter what happened, it wasn't your fault. He had no right—"

"I thought about not going, but there was something inside of me that had already given in. Just keep the other parts of your life clean, I told myself, and do what you have to do to get by until the end of the semester. So I did." She looked up at me and her eyes were red and wet. Tears ran down her cheeks and dripped from her chin. "That fucker," she whispered. "That goddamned fucker."

I didn't know what to do, so I stood there quietly, listening to Lucy cry into her hands. I don't know how long it lasted, ten minutes or half an hour, but gradually the ferocity of her crying diminished and she lowered her hands from her face.

"I could really use a smoke and a beer," she finally said. "How 'bout it?"

Chapter Ten

Sitting on the floor of Charles Coker's office, we smoked and drank beer and ate cold pizza. Gradually Lucy's mood brightened, and I could see some of the good fuck-you come back into her eyes, some of the bad fuck-you leave.

She asked me about my family, and I told her about my mom and my dad back in Pennsylvania. She listened intently, and I found myself a little bit surprised that she'd be interested at all. I'd assumed that I was just a diversion for her. We talked about high school, though she seemed unwilling to share some details, and I didn't push. I didn't want to ruin her mood.

"Oh God," Lucy finally said, dropping a half-eaten slice of pizza back into the box. "If I eat any more I'll die. I swear to God, Paul."

I was leaning back on my arms, looking at her, and had been doing so for about the last five minutes. Now she noticed and said, "What are you looking at?"

Heat immediately blossomed in my face and I said, "Nothing. Sorry."

She clapped a hand dramatically over her heart and said, "Nothing? That's awful! I'm shattered. And here I thought you were looking at *me*."

I smiled. "Okay, fine. So I was looking at you. I didn't mean to stare. Just let me go with a warning this time, okay, officer?"

Lucy shook a finger sternly at me, but was still smiling. She stood up, knees popping, and stretched her back, arching like a cat, arms extended over her head, fingers interlaced. Her shirt rode up and I caught a glimpse of her stomach, saw how her low-slung jeans rested on the smooth bumps of her hip bones. Instinctively I turned away, face flaring. When I looked back, Lucy had walked to the bookshelf behind Coker's desk and was looking through the titles.

"Aha," she said to herself, and pulled one of the books, a thin leather-bound volume, from the shelf. She turned to me. "Come over here," she said, and patted Coker's chair.

I sat down in the leather swivel chair and Lucy pushed it back as far away from the desk as it would go, until I felt my head resting against the wall. Then she sat down on the front edge of the desk, just a couple of feet from me, the book still in her hand.

"What's that?" I asked.

She held it up so I could see the title engraved in gold on the front. *A Connecticut Yankee in King Arthur's Court*, by Mark Twain. She opened the cover and showed me the first page, which was marked with handwritten black script. "It's signed, as you can see, by Twain himself. I asked Coker once, if it was worth so much, why he didn't keep it locked in a safe, or at least hidden. He looked at me like I was simple and said, 'Books are meant to be read, Lucy, not hidden away out of sight.' Charles reads this particular book once a year, right around Christmas. This year I think he'll have himself a little surprise, though."

"Wait," I said. "You're not going to take it, are you?" From what Lucy had told me, it wouldn't be too hard for Coker to figure out who had broken into his office. And if he called the police and they searched her room.... But Lucy was shaking her head, and I felt at least some relief.

79

"No, no," she said. "I'm not a thief."

I felt pressure between my legs and looked down. Lucy's foot was propped on the edge of the chair. Immediately I felt myself stir. When I looked back at her, the sly, mischievous expression that I had already come to associate with Lucy was back on her face.

"The question now, Paul," she said, "is whether you're willing to help me." She paused and held my gaze until I had to look down. "Are you?"

I swallowed and heard a dry click from my throat. "What do you want me to do?"

She shrugged. "Not much. Just sit there. Can you do that? For me?"

I nodded.

"Good." She slid off the edge of desk and knelt between my legs, slid her hands up my thighs, massaged me through my jeans. I rested my head back against the wall as she worked my button and fly, felt a flutter in my stomach as she pulled me free.

As she stroked me, her fingers cool and gentle, teasing, she whispered, "This time I want you to tell me when, okay?"

I closed my eyes and found her hair with my hands. As she moved we found a rhythm, and I felt the pressure growing in my head and in my groin and said, "Lucy —"

Her mouth was suddenly gone but her hand kept going, and my hips thrust forward of their own volition and I emptied, trembling, unable to stop the jittering of my legs, back, neck, and shoulders, tight and hunched. When I finally could I looked down, and Lucy was smiling up at me, her lips moist, her hair tousled from my fingers.

In her hand she held Coker's signed copy of *A Connecticut Yankee in King Arthur's Court*, open to the dedication page. Breathing a contented sigh, Lucy clapped the book shut and stood, leaned over me, and replaced the book on the shelf.

Stooping over, she planted her hands on the armrests of the chair and kissed me on the mouth.

"Thank you, Paul," she whispered into my ear. "That was a nice thing for you to do."

There were absolutely no words for me to say, so I didn't say anything. We left the pizza box and empty beer bottles and left the office.

***

As I lay down to sleep that night, back in Smith, listening to the muffled sound of the wind as it screamed around the corner of the dorm, I felt guilty for what we'd done. And I felt afraid. Not of Coker, not of being found out, not of how I'd feel the next time I saw Lucy, not of having to look at myself in the mirror tomorrow. I was scared not of what I'd done, but of what I might do next time, whatever that meant.

I dreamed that night, and the dreams weren't good…I know because I woke up soaked in sweat, the covers kicked to the bottom of the bed. The one thing I remembered was Lucy, her mouth close to my ear, urgently whispering words I couldn't understand.

Years and years later, I would finally start to realize what she was asking me for.

CHAPTER ELEVEN

I got home around midnight from my meeting with Steve, eased my way silently into the bedroom, and fumbled my clothes off in the dark. Dottie was asleep and her breathing was soft and normal, interrupted every now and then by a gentle snore. Wearing only my boxer shorts, I lay down next to her and laced my fingers together beneath my head, the way I'd slept since I was a kid. I was tired and expected sleep to come quickly, but it didn't. An hour later, my mind still working, I got up again.

I opened the door to Naomi's bedroom, and the wedge of light from the hallway revealed her sleeping form nestled snugly beneath her down comforter. Over our drinks, Steve had commented on how quickly life went by, and that soon my own daughter would be in college. Those thoughts had occurred to me thousands of times over her life, of course, but not in the way I felt Steve had meant it, if not on the surface, then underneath.

Soon, he seemed to have been saying to me, she'll be in the same place we were, and who knows what will happen when she gets there, who she'll meet, what he'll do to her. Looking at my daughter, my heart beat so hard it felt like it would come bulging out of my mouth, and I realized that I was terrified, both for her and for myself. I was scared of the things that could happen to a young girl, and I knew that if anyone ever hurt her the way Lucy had been hurt, I would kill that person with my own bare hands.

The reality that I wasn't thinking rationally became clear to me then, and I saw that I hadn't been operating on the same wavelength as the rest of the world since Steve called. In my mind, Naomi's boyfriend Nathan had already taken advantage of her, left her hurt and depleted, half the girl she had been. But Nathan wouldn't do that. I knew Nathan, and I knew his parents. Good people who had raised a good son. A sound of disgust rose up my throat and tried to come out, but I covered my mouth and swallowed it.

My mind cycled back to the argument Dottie and I had gotten into that morning, and suddenly everything about how I'd acted was repulsive to me. I knew Naomi wasn't the kind of girl who would dress in trashy clothes, who wanted to advertise herself to the pack of horny teenage boys at the mall or at school, knew beyond a shadow of a doubt that she was savvier than her friends, full of more common sense than I'd had at her age. But I also knew that it wasn't always about who a young woman was, how she saw the world, the way she treated others. Lucy had taught me that, and my first lesson had come that night in Coker's office. Sometimes — *too many times* — it wasn't about you at all; it was what other people wanted from you, and how skillful they could be about getting it. Even if it wasn't Nathan, it would be someone, eventually. It always was.

Suddenly and irrationally I wished that I would be dead and gone before I had to see my daughter hurt that way. It was selfish and it was weak, but I felt both of those things. I couldn't believe any father would wish otherwise, but maybe I was wrong. Maybe there were fathers out there who thought they could protect their children, save them from the monsters that wanted to hurt them behind doors closed to the rest of the world. But that couldn't be done. At some point, Naomi would be alone, no matter how carefully I watched her.

I pulled her door shut again and walked into the kitchen and put water on to boil, trying to stop the tremor that had taken over my hands. When the electric kettle clicked off, I brewed myself a mug of chamomile tea, then sat at the kitchen table sipping it slowly, hearing the sound of the grandfather clock ticking its metronomic cadence in the living room, the wind whistling around the corner of the house.

I wasn't surprised that Steve's words that night had brought this sleeplessness, this disturbance, upon me, but at the same time, I was shocked by the power of having seen him again after so many years. It was like seeing something in real life that had previously existed only in a book or a very vivid recurring dream. A nightmare. That he was real flesh and blood, a walking, talking man just like me, seemed incongruous with the reality I'd been living all these years.

Mostly, what he'd seemed intent on doing as we sat in the bar was rehashing the good times, before Pennsylvania, before the fire. I'd been fine with that, for a while anyway, but as the minutes ticked into an hour and then two, I started to see what was behind Steve's eyes, a fearful, even terrified presence. As he talked, I noticed a pattern in his speech. Everything he said to me lacked an ending. He was like a man stepping repeatedly to the edge of a cliff, the water hundreds of feet below, telling himself, "I can do this, I can do this," and then backing off each time, only to come back moments later to the same spot, telling himself the same thing.

And so I continued to listen, hoping that Steve would soon step to the edge and jump. Once I thought he almost had.

Smoking his tenth or twelfth cigarette since we'd met up, Steve had looked at me over his steepled fingers. In the low light of the bar, his face, which I had at first thought seemed too thin to fit the young man I had once known, seemed drawn and almost cadaverous.

"Paul," he said, then paused, looked at his hands, at the burning ember of the cigarette. "Man, Paul, it's like these things happen to you, these *fucked up things*, and for the rest of your life you're the person you are because of fifteen minutes that weren't even your fault, you know? I mean, what do you *do* with that?"

When I didn't answer he continued, his voice low and conspiratorial, like someone might overhear us and know what we were talking about after all these years. "I mean, don't you think about it? The fire?"

Honestly, I answered, "Not really. I used to, and then, I don't know when, it just stopped. I think about Lucy sometimes, about why Roscoe did it, but it's yesterday's news. I kind of got to the point where I thought, okay, there was a fire, Lucy died. It's horrible, but it was no one's fault. It just happened. Why dwell on it?"

Steve slapped his hands on the table. He'd had too much to drink, and I was glad he wouldn't be driving. "How can that be true, man?! Shit, I mean, don't you think about what you could have done? What would have happened if you'd stopped her before she left the barn, or if she never came to the farm at all?"

I nodded slowly, seeing a man in front of me who didn't just want to talk about old times, but rather a man who was seeking an exculpation that neither I nor anyone else would ever be able to give him. I felt an urge to say to him that once I too had sought that door out of the labyrinth, but in the end the only way to escape was to convince myself that escape wasn't really a possibility. When I got right down to brass tacks, all I could really do was give up and make the labyrinth my own, to fill it with all the things I loved the most, and then learn to live in it as normally as possible.

But I couldn't say those things to him; he wouldn't have understood what I meant. Hell, maybe I didn't even believe the words myself.

In the end, I think what really had me awake that night was that none of what happened to Lucy and Roscoe had been Steve's fault. None of it. If anyone was to blame for Lucy's death, it was me. And no matter how I tried to think my way through a thousand different scenarios, I couldn't reason out a way he could blame himself for what happened to me or Roscoe or Lucy.

So why had he come calling?

CHAPTER TWELVE

The next morning, feeling groggy and unable to focus on anything right in front of me, I called in sick to work at the magazine and told Dottie I'd be back before dinner. The look of concern on her face was obvious, and I couldn't blame her; I knew I was acting strangely.

"Everything's fine," I said, and gave her a kiss. "This isn't about yesterday. I know I was a jerk."

Naomi walked into the kitchen and poured herself a bowl of cereal, then sat down at the breakfast bar to eat. With her hair pulled back in a ponytail, wearing a pair of worn jeans and a gray Gap hoodie, she looked more beautiful than I'd ever seen her, and I felt a pang of sadness in my chest. She *was* pretty, not only in the eyes of me, her father, but really beautiful. Her entire life, she would have to carry that.

"Want a ride to school?" I asked her, kissing the top of her head. Her still-damp hair smelled like shampoo and left my lips wet. My thoughts from last night danced malignantly at the edges of my mind, but I stonewalled them the best I could.

She looked up at me. "You aren't going to work?"

"Not today. Got to do a couple of things."

"Cool," she said. "I hate the bus. Let me just grab my books."

87

After dropping Naomi at school, I headed toward the city and pulled into the parking lot of the airport Marriott. At the desk, I asked the attendant to ring Steve's room, but they told me he had checked out already.

"God, really?" I said. "I was supposed to meet him here this morning. Is there any way you can give me his phone number or address?"

The young woman gave me a look out of the corner of her eye and told me it was against hotel policy to share that kind of information. Feeling awkward and stalker-ish, I left the hotel and stood outside, thinking about what to do and why I felt so compelled to do anything at all.

What it came down to was the simple fact that Steve had made the trip from wherever he lived out here to Pennsylvania, presumably to tell me something that had been working in his mind for years. If I hadn't been so shocked by his call and then by the uncomfortable nature of our meeting last night, I would have seen it sooner. In a very real way, I now realized, our conversation the previous evening had felt like an abortive suicide note. Steve had sounded like a man who wanted to make sure *someone* understood why he had chosen to take his own life. I could picture it. At the funeral, so-and-so would say, *He always seemed so happy. Why do you think he did it?* And I would have the answer. I would look to make sure Dorothy was out of earshot, then say, *He blamed himself for the death of a girl we both loved. I don't think he ever got over it.*

Those words sticking in my mind, I rushed back into the hotel and found the business center just off the lobby. I sat down at one of the terminals in the cluster and navigated to a search engine, then typed in Steve's name. He had given me next to no information about what he did or where he lived, and that now seemed like a deliberate act on his part.

The search turned up thousands of entries for Steve Jones,

and I leaned back in my chair, drumming my fingers on the desk and wishing Naomi was there to help. When it came to word processing programs, I was fairly competent, but beyond that I was largely computer illiterate, a fact my coworkers at the magazine never let me live down.

A teenaged girl dressed in black with braided black hair was sitting at a computer across from me. She had an earbud attached to an iPod dangling from one ear, but the one facing me was free.

"Excuse me," I said, and when she didn't react, I said it again.

"Me?" she said, looking over her shoulder, then back at me. She pulled the earbud free and set her iPod down on the desk.

I nodded at her. "Maybe you can help me with something."

"Maybe," she said, but I could see that she was wary of me. *Good for you*, I thought. *You* should *be wary of creepy old guys.*

"I'm trying to find a friend of mine on the Internet, but I haven't seen him for a while and I don't know much about what he's doing now. Any ideas? I'm sorry to bug you with this, but I figured you'd probably know more than me about how to do this kind of thing."

"Oh," she said, standing and coming over to my desk. "Sure, no biggie. Can I sit there?"

I stood and let her take my seat, then stood behind her, not so close she'd feel like I was trying to sneak a peek down the front of her shirt.

"Okay," she said. "So you were in the right place. What's his name?"

I told her and she punched it in. "Anything else you can tell me about him?"

For a moment I struggled to think of something, but I drew a blank. "No, not really. We went to college together, but I haven't really talked with him much since then."

She smiled. "Bingo. What college?"

"Penton College, in Ohio," I said.

She typed Penton and Ohio into the search engine and then clicked on the link to the school's website. Once there, she clicked a couple more times, too fast for me to see, and a new page popped up. It read: ALUMNI CONNECTION. Below that, a hyperlink offered an alumni directory. She clicked into the directory and typed Steve's name in, and when she was given a choice between three men named Steve Jones, asked me what year he'd graduated and clicked on the appropriate link. A moment later Steve's information came up on the screen.

STEVEN ALEXANDER JONES.

ADDRESS: 3167 WALNUT LATE DANBURY, OH 43012

EMAIL: STEVE.JONES2@Z-MAIL.NET

"There," the girl said, getting up. "Cake."

I thanked her and she went back to her own computer, plugged her earbuds back in, both this time, and did her level best to show how successfully she had forgotten I existed.

After writing down the info the girl had found, I left and went back out to my car. I sat there, the engine off. This was ridiculous. What Steve had done was the worst kind of intrusion. What gave a man the right to insert himself back into the life of an acquaintance he hadn't seen in nearly twenty years? My balance had been thrown off, and I wanted to recover some sense of normalcy. To do that, I thought I needed to talk to Steve again. I started the engine and drove straight home.

Naomi was still at school and Dottie was out somewhere, leaving me alone in the house. I sat down at my computer and navigated to my email, tapped in the address from the information scribbled on the scrap of paper from the info center, and then sat still, thinking about what to write.

I typed: *Steve, when we got together last night, you seemed down, and when I woke up this morning I was worried about you. I hope this is your current email address. If it is, would you please write me back with your phone number so I can give you a call?*

Your friend,
Paul.

When I'd sent the note, I went into the kitchen and poured myself a glass of orange juice, then sat down in one of the comfortable chairs in the living room. I tried to reason my way through the situation with Steve, but my mind seemed incapable of focusing for long, and in minutes my thoughts returned to that first year at Penton.

For so many years I'd struggled to condition myself to shunt these thoughts into a safe place when they came up, but now I found myself incapable of refusing them. I didn't want to anymore. In some way, it felt very much as though I'd been waiting for this to happen, for something to come back into my life after so long, a catalyst to start this process. Now it had, and I wasn't sure what to do with it.

I glanced at the clock on the DVD player and saw that it was just after ten o'clock. If I left now, I could be in New York by noon, home by four or five, maybe even before Dottie got home. A simple up-and-back trip.

I stood and went to my desk, scribbled a quick note on a legal pad telling Dottie where I was going, then put the note on the kitchen counter in a place where she wouldn't be able to miss it.

I'd been to see Roscoe dozens of times over the years and had never looked forward to the visits, but this time I felt an unfamiliar excitement in my chest. I was going to see my old friend, the one real link I'd had all these years to the way things had been once.

As I backed the car out of the driveway and headed toward I-95, my thoughts turned back to 1985 with equal measures of anticipation and dread.

PART II

Mid-Semester Break. Anything for Money.
Making Movies.

CHAPTER THIRTEEN

When I woke up the next morning at eight-thirty, I lay in bed listening for the sounds to which I'd become so accustomed over the last two months. The squeak of the top bunk as Roscoe shifted in his sleep. Muttered conversations in the hallway outside as my floor-mates wandered zombie-like toward towards the nearest source of coffee. Doors opening and closing as students trundled in and out of the dining hall two stories below our window.

But I heard none of those things.

Instead, I heard new sounds. My own breathing. A dripping from the bathroom, the sink probably. Birds.

And then I saw something completely different: Coker's office in a shambles, the framed picture of his family lying shattered on the floor, the empty pizza box and beer bottles scattered about. For a second I was literally stiff with terror, then I caught myself and forced my body to relax. *It's okay*, I told myself, *there's no way for him to know it was me and Lucy. No way.*

Still struggling to shrug off the last of the anxiety, I rose and showered, threw on a pair of jeans and a flannel shirt, and went downstairs for breakfast. There were still enough students around that the college had to keep one or two of the dining halls open, and, lucky me, the one open for breakfast was in Smith. I loaded my plate up with bacon and eggs and filled one of the tiny ceramic mugs with scalding hot coffee, then found myself a place to sit near the wall. As I ate, I thought about Lucy and what we'd done last night.

More than anything else, I found — and this came as a surprise to me, especially considering the feeling I'd woken with — that I was coming to terms in a grudging sort of way with what had happened. I'd crossed more than one of the ethical lines behind which I'd always stood in the past, but if I didn't feel wonderful about what we'd done, I didn't exactly feel terrible, either. It wasn't like we'd vandalized a convent; Coker was an immoral asshole, a professor who had abused his position by manipulating a young girl into sex. He deserved what he'd gotten. Worse, even.

Having finished my breakfast, I found that I wasn't ready at this early hour to sit down in front of my cranky old typewriter and crank on my new story. Since I'd finally gotten on the proverbial horse — my IBM Selectric, in this case — and started to ride, I had discovered that while the morning was the richest time of the day for me in terms of my imagination, it was the worst time of the day for me to work. Rather, I preferred to see where my thoughts would take me and refine as much as I could inside my head, then spend an hour or two in the evening getting it all down on paper.

So I decided to take a walk.

I stood outside the front door of Smith, smoking and trying to figure out where I wanted to go. Not into town. I'd already eaten, so the Hamburger Inn — where you could get two greasy burgers, an enormous pile of fries, and all the coffee you could drink for two-fifty — held no attraction. Neither did Rutherford's, the bookstore. Small town Ohio boasted hard-working, salt-of-the-earth people, but when it came to the range of books they considered "literature," most of the citizens were still stuck somewhere in the 1920's. After a couple of minutes of intercranial back and forth, I decided to start walking and see where I ended up.

Smoking one cigarette after another — I'd managed to become remarkably addicted to the things in two short months — I made my way across the residential side of campus, passing a few students who were also stranded at school for break. At Sandusky Street I stopped to wait for the traffic signal to turn, and saw the lights.

In front of Sturges Hall, a Penton PD cruiser sat idling, roof lights flashing. My stomach cramped immediately, and I fought the ridiculous urge to turn and run the other way. Instead, I crossed the street when the light turned green — *just a student taking a walk*, I told myself, *nothing to hide* — and strolled up the main path toward the academic buildings, a path that would take me past Sturges Hall. This was what I had come to see, after all; the very idea that my little walk had been aimless was laughable.

As I approached the building, the front doors opened and two men emerged. One was a cop. He wore an obligatory smile, and even from where I was I could see the boredom in his eyes. The other man I recognized from the picture I'd seen last night on his desk, the one of him and his family. Charles Coker. He was older than he'd looked in the photograph, his hair more salt and pepper now than brown, his beard shot through with patches of gray. There was none of the youthful virility I'd expected after Lucy's story; instead, he looked tired and stooped, more defeated than angry. He looked like a man who had half expected something like this to happen, just because that's how college kids were.

Behind him, the door opened again and a woman followed Coker and the cop out onto the steps. It was Coker's wife, the pretty blonde, her face creased with concern. She hurried down the stairs and put her hands on Coker's arm as if to restrain him. He tried to shrug her off, but she wouldn't let go. As I watched, she turned her face toward his ear and whispered something. At first he shook his head, then he closed his eyes for a moment and put his hand over his wife's, nodding.

"Do you think you'll find these little shits?" he asked the cop.

The cop shook his head. "Honestly, I doubt it. With these kinds of things, you catch them going in or out. Give me just a second." He reached through the rolled-down window of the police cruiser and picked up the CB handset. "Polly, looks like there *was* a break-in up here. I'm going to bring the guy down to make a report, over." He turned to Coker and said, "Hop in. Let's take a ride down to the station."

I passed by as Coker got into the car, and for a moment I wasn't ten feet from the man. I felt a pang of fresh guilt. Coker didn't *look* like a monster, like a man capable of doing the things Lucy had described. Had she told me the truth? I already knew how manipulative she could be. Could I rightfully be shocked if everything she'd led me into last night had been some kind of ruse? What if Coker had done no more than give Lucy a C when she thought she'd deserved an A?

I shoved my hands into my pockets and put my head down, feeling not for the first time like I had all too willingly walked into a situation that could do nothing but hurt me.

***

Seeing Coker got me thinking about Lucy. She was beautiful — there was no denying that — but I'd never met anyone more unpredictable. Unlike Roscoe, whose escapades had more to do with pure carnal appetite, everything Lucy did seemed part of some complex internal plan she would never share with anyone else…if she even *knew* she was following it at all, that was. This made her both attractive and dangerous, but I couldn't deny that my desire to see her and be around her was stronger than ever. If anything, what we had done last night had only served to make her more accessible to me. I wanted to know more. Legs beginning to feel rubbery, I set off to find Steve, the only person I knew with any link to Lucy at all.

As I passed by the Sigma Theta house, a big, blocky brick building like all of the other fraternity houses on the Penton campus, I glanced over at it, expecting to see that it too had been deserted for the weekend, but to my surprise there were still a few cars parked in the lot. I scanned the windows on the second floor, counting over from the right, and located Steve's, which was open. When Roscoe and I went out, we generally ended up in Steve's room, and although I had come to college with no intention of going Greek, I'd gotten to know Steve well enough that the idea had been planted in my head. I knew that when bids were extended at the end of the semester, I would get one; I just didn't know what I'd do about it yet.

Cupping my hands around my mouth, I called out, "Steve!" Almost immediately he appeared in the window, looking ruffled and wearing a frown on his usually cheerful face. He saw me and ducked his head back into the room, exchanged a few words with someone, and then re-emerged.

"Come on up, Paul. The combination for the door is seven-five-five." He ducked back out of the window and I walked to the back door of the house.

I went in through one of the two back doors, both of which opened into stairwells, and was immediately assaulted by the piss smell that would always define the house in my mind. It was strongest in the stairwells because the brothers, when they were too drunk, too tired, or just too lazy, would often take a leak into one of the large gray trashcans just inside the stairwell doors on each level. I'd seen this happen often enough to understand that it was an accepted ritual, but even after I moved into the house the following year, I could never bring myself to do it.

I made my way up the stairs and pushed through the chipped and dented green door into the second floor hallway. The hall ran down the center of the house, and doors lined each side at twelve-foot intervals.

Every door had its own design, put there by the current occupant. One of the brothers, a true Californian stoner named Billy Keeler, had painted an amazingly detailed mural of the Grim Reaper standing over a sleeping, nude blonde woman. Inside, I knew that his walls continued the story, the painting just as exquisite.

Joe Reid, the president of the fraternity, had scrawled two simple words in black on his white door. OVAL OFFICE.

Steve's door was my favorite, though.

A film student, Steve had taken his favorite scenes from maybe twenty different movies and rendered them in comic-strip size on the door, speech captions and all. It must have taken him days or even weeks of neck-cramping work, but when you mentioned it to Steve, he just nodded and went back to whatever he was drinking or smoking at the time. That was Steve.

Arriving at his door, I knocked. After a moment, Steve opened the door, and I saw the last thing I'd expected.

CHAPTER FOURTEEN

Stepping into Steve's room, I noticed two things immediately. The first was that Steve was a wreck. Normally he was impeccable in terms of his personal appearance, his brown hair longish but neatly parted on the left, his clothes clean and well-tended. The young man I saw in front of me now might as well have been the stoned, grungy brother of the Steve I knew. He wore a pair of grimy jeans with rips at both knees and a stained white T-shirt. His hair stuck up at odd angles, and at least two or three days-worth of stubble peppered his cheeks.

And Roscoe was sitting on the brown leather couch next to the window. I felt like someone had backhanded me.

"Roscoe," I said, fighting an off-kilter feeling in my head. "I thought you went home."

He was holding a bottle of PBR, and instead of answering me, he raised the bottle to his lips and took a long swallow.

"Come on in, man," Steve said, moving out of the doorway. The air was thick with whatever they'd been talking about; I was painfully aware that I had stumbled on something I shouldn't have.

I sat down in the chair in front of Steve's desk, a desk that was, normally, obsessively organized. Today, drifts of paper covered almost the entire surface, and more sloughed off the edge and onto the floor. The wastebasket was full of wadded sheets, and a host of other crumpled balls lay where they had fallen.

Roscoe was lighting a cigarette.

"What's going on, man?" I said. I'd never seen him this way, sullen, despondent. I started to feel more than confused, something closer to afraid. When he didn't answer me, I looked up at Steve. He shrugged and sat down on the couch next to Roscoe.

"Want a beer?" he asked me.

"Sure."

Steve leaned over to open the mini-fridge next to the couch. He handed me the cold bottle and I twisted the top off and took a drink.

When nobody spoke, I said, "So is anyone going to tell me what's going on here, or do I have to start guessing?" I tried to smile and keep my tone light, but failed at both.

Roscoe turned to blow smoke out of the window and I saw the faint red marks on his neck, just above the collar of his shirt, and on his temple. His left eye was discolored with a fading bruise, not so that I'd noticed when I first walked in, but it must have hurt like a bastard when it happened.

I slipped my own pack of smokes from the inside pocket of my jacket and lit one, then leaned back in the chair and waited. In his face I could see reflected the turbulent thoughts crashing and building and swirling in his brain, and I wanted to leave, to pace, to not have shown up in the first place. But I just sat quietly, and finally Roscoe spoke.

"I *did* go home," he said. He sounded toneless and artificial, like a machine speaking words. "I went home, and when I got there, my dad met me at the front door with a two-by-four."

My head swam. Never had Roscoe spoken of trouble at home. Never. But then I thought about how little conversation we'd actually *had* about home. Beyond the details—names, number of siblings (in his case, one brother, older and out of the house for years)—he'd never brought it up.

"Why?" I said. "Why would he do that?"

Roscoe shook his head and propped his beer between his legs. He finally looked at me, and when I saw the wetness of his eyes, it wrenched me so powerfully that I for a moment I couldn't breathe.

Only later, once I was alone, did the true source of that feeling become obvious to me. Yes, it was because Roscoe's father had attacked him, and yes, it was because this person sitting in front of me now seemed so different from the guy I'd grown to love. But mostly, and selfishly, it was because I was afraid. Not just for Roscoe, but for myself. I was afraid that Roscoe's father had permanently taken away the person who had made me, on so many occasions, happy.

When Roscoe only shrugged at my question, I said, "Is this the first time?"

A sound welled up from Roscoe's chest and into his mouth, and it took me a second to recognize it for what it was: a laugh. "No," he said, his voice thick. "Not the first time. Not the second time. You get the idea." He caught my eyes again, and I saw the defeat there, saw so clearly that I wanted to scream at myself the reasons why Roscoe was who he was, why he drank and smoked and screwed anyone who would go home with him. I understood more in those few seconds than I think Roscoe would understand for most of his own life.

His uncanny skill when it came to seeing the true nature of others, for instance. When you lived with someone who at any moment might decide it was a good time to brand your skin raw and red with a belt or swing at your head with a slab of wood, I'm sure reading the things *behind the eyes* became second-nature. And the way he could turn a bad, maybe even a terrible situation into a manageable one; that also made sense.

I remembered how he had treated me earlier in the semester when I had simply wanted to crawl into a hole and die after the party at the abandoned mansion, how he had simply made me feel better when I thought nothing could. Why was a kid with an abusive parent (maybe two, who knew? The one time I'd talked to his mother, she'd sounded drunk) a master of negotiation and pacification, a handler?

"I understand why you didn't tell me," I said.

Roscoe nodded and looked back out the window. With the back of one hand, he wiped at his eyes. "Thanks," he said.

There was silence again for a moment, and then Steve pushed himself back off the couch and went to his chest-of-drawers. When he turned around, he was holding a plastic Baggie stuffed with green.

"Everything's gonna feel a lot better in about...," he looked down at his watch, "ten minutes. You guys down?"

As Steve set about packing his bong, I dropped into his desk chair and looked at Roscoe. He was still gazing out the window and plucking at his lower lip with his thumb and forefinger, and I tried to think back over the past several months. Had there ever been signs? I didn't think so, but I'd been so caught up recently with my own problems and school, and now Lucy, that Bigfoot could have come up to me to bum a smoke and all I'd have said was sure, need a light?

And then the bleak truth of it all broke through the hardpan surface of my brain. and I saw what had been hidden in front of me, in plain sight, since the very first time I'd met Roscoe. There were no signs because everything about him, everything he said and everything he did, was testament to what he'd been through. When you look at a building, you don't see one stone or brick.

Then Steve handed me the bong, and after a while I forgot to think about any of the bad stuff, and that was fine with me.

102

***

Three hours later I barely knew what planet I was on. Steve had reloaded the bong time after time, and the beer he'd had stashed in the fridge was a distant memory. I'd moved to the floor and sat with my back against the wall, feeling alternately high and drunk, praying I wouldn't get the spins and barf all over Steve's carpet.

After an indeterminate amount of liquid time, I looked up and found both Steve and Roscoe asleep, Steve in his chair, Roscoe on the couch, snoring, his head propped against the windowsill. Knowing that I only had a few minutes to work with before I joined them, I jerked to my feet and headed back to Smith.

***

The sun was warm on my face and chest when I woke up late the next morning.

Roscoe is back.

The events of the previous day rushed back into my hangover; Roscoe's father, the marks on his neck and face. The anger that had coursed through me so powerfully the day before returned, but steadier now, a low thrum in my head and chest.

On the bunk above me Roscoe snorted in his sleep, and then turned onto his side or back, causing the springs to creak. I hadn't heard him come in last night, or if I had, I'd forgotten all about it.

"Stop moving around so much," I heard an unfamiliar voice whisper, and Roscoe grunted something back. After a while, the breathing coming from above me leveled out, and I thought it would be safe to move.

Moving gingerly, I rose, showered, and headed downstairs for breakfast.

By the time Roscoe wandered through the door of the cafeteria at around a quarter to ten, most of the other students who'd shown for breakfast had emptied out. I would long ago have been gone too except for the fact that I'd brought *Bleak*

House with me, and had been struggling through the same three pages for the last forty-five minutes. As was usually the case the day after I smoked too much pot, my attention kept wandering, a problem compounded by the fact that I'd read more entertaining prose on the back of shampoo bottles.

I watched as Roscoe moved through the serving line, scooping himself a mammoth portion of the rubbery, too-yellow eggs, then filling the remaining area on his plate with sausage patties and strips of shriveled bacon. He stopped to get himself coffee, and then came over to the table where I was sitting.

"Morning, fuckface," he said, collapsing into his chair, and I smiled, not just at the words, but also at his voice when he'd said them. Whatever was going on in his head — and I knew there had to be things I couldn't even begin to comprehend — he'd put them aside. Or maybe I just fooled myself into hearing what I wanted to hear because it was easier that way. I don't know. What I do know is that in his voice I heard the old Roscoe, and it made me happy.

"When'd you get back to the room?" I asked. "I didn't hear you come in."

He shrugged and shoved an impossibly gelatinous clump of egg into his mouth. "Not the foggiest fucking idea, Paco. Whatever we smoked last night, it chopped me down. I remember being in Steve's room, then I was outside, and then I woke up next to what's-her-face. Julia, I think. Or Jessica. She said we got together at Phi Psi, but that was news to me." He shoveled some more eggs into his face and bit off the end of a slice of bacon, then washed the mixture down with a slug of coffee. If he was preoccupied by anything, it didn't show in his demeanor. The bruise around his eye was almost unnoticeable. "So," he said when he'd swallowed the load, "what do you think about the movie idea?"

"Movie idea?"

"Last night? Steve's project?" Roscoe moved his hands in

little windmill motions, trying to encourage my memory.

"I'm sorry, man, but I have *no idea* what you're talking about."

Roscoe blew out through his teeth and leaned back in his chair, taking another sip of coffee. "Okay, quick version, Paco. For his senior thesis, Steve's making a movie. So he sits around for a couple of weeks trying to write a script, but he can't come up with a solid idea. In the end, all he has to this point is about two reams of trash."

I remembered the drifts of paper on the desk, the litter of crumpled balls on the floor. A vague recollection of a conversation drifted into my brain. Not *what* had been said, just that something had.

"He should get someone to help him with the script," I said.

"Funny you should say that, Paco. That's exactly what you said last night, right before you told Steve that you were a creative writing major and that you had this *great* idea for a story. On top of all that, you said you thought this story would translate *wonderfully* — your word. I nearly died laughing, you fairy — to the screen. By the time you were done, Steve was practically coming in his pants."

"I said that?" I asked.

He nodded and drank more coffee. "You did indeed, my friend." Looking down at his watch, Roscoe grunted. "In fact, you're supposed to meet him up at Sigma Theta in about fifteen minutes to get started on the script."

***

When I got up to the house, I found Steve sitting in front of his desk, drinking a beer. He'd tidied the room a bit since the night before, and he had a stick of incense burning in a holder on the coffee table. When I walked in, he looked at me almost bashfully, and I immediately understood that it was killing him to need help with this project. That he was a senior and I was a freshman probably didn't help matters much.

105

"What's the dilly, Paul?" he said as I sat down on the couch. "Get a beer if you want." Since a beer was the last thing in the world I wanted, I shook my head. "So what's this idea of yours?"

I took a deep breath, then lit up a smoke. "I was thinking about how this would look like as a movie on the way over. Some parts are easy, just two guys talking to each other in a cabin, that kind of thing. There's a lot of that in the beginning. There are these two brothers and their father has just died, so they head out to the cabin in the mountains where they used to go during breaks from school to really say goodbye right. They get shithouse drunk and find out that their father had molested them both, threatening to hurt the other brother if either ever told. It's too much for the younger brother to handle and he wants to leave, so they get into the Jeep and take off. They're both wasted, so you know nothing good is going to happen. All that's just talking. Other parts, though...."

"Other parts?" Steve said, making a go-ahead gesture with his hands.

I nodded. "It's going to be tough. The premise of the story is that the two brothers are taken captive by these...people-farming cannibals who live in the mountains. Their Jeep runs off the road that night when they're drunk and trying to leave the cabin, and when someone finally comes along, it's the wrong guys. That's bad enough. But the really bad part is that there are no fertile males left among the human livestock the cannibals already have, so they make one of the brothers...well, you know. It's all about making babies, and they don't have a stud because of inbreeding. Then these two guys fall into their laps and it looks like all their problems are solved."

Steve chuckled and took a sip of beer. "That's fucking sick, man."

I nodded. "It's going to be the hardest scene. Everything else is pretty typical horror stuff, but the scene where they force the kid to, you know, *mate* with one of the women...it's bad. One of the hillbillies has a knife to his brother's neck, ready to kill him if he can't go through with it."

"So he has to fuck one of the inbred women in front of an audience, knowing that if he can't get it up, his brother's hamburger?"

"Yeah." I felt like crawling under the couch.

"I have to ask you a question, man," Steve said, shaking his head. "How does it feel to *think* of something like that?"

I laughed. "Not great. I've been pretty embarrassed about it for a while now." I took a drag from my cigarette, then said, "What do you think?"

"Fuckin' cool, man," he said. "I mean, it's not *normal* that you thought of it, but it's cool."

"You don't think it's too out there?"

He laughed. "Maybe, but you know, fuck 'em if they can't take a joke. Better than anything I came up with."

I shrugged. "Your funeral."

"Yeah," he said, leaning over to grab a couple of beers from his fridge. "Maybe. But I'm going to make sure everyone knows you're the sick bastard who came up with it."

CHAPTER FIFTEEN

It didn't take us a week to write the script for Steve's short film; it took us two. Two weeks of going to class each day, of walking to the academic buildings from the residential side of campus early in the morning, then trudging home as night fell, cold even in my coat and the heavy L.L. Bean flannel shirts my parents had ordered and sent to me for my birthday. We got our first snow of the year, an inch and a half two weeks before Thanksgiving Break, and after that it hadn't stopped coming. Not a lot, but every couple of days a new layer would drift to the ground, dry and shifting, like ash.

After class I'd dump my books in the room and then head up to Steve's. When we finished with slamming the fried crap the house cook had prepared that evening down our throats, we would head up to Steve's room and put a serious hurting on the beer he had stowed away in his fridge, type up what we'd gotten done over dinner, and then revise what we already had.

By the time a week and a half had passed, we were both exhausted, and I found myself stumbling around each day in a hungover haze. Whatever my parents had had in mind for me when they sent me off to college, I was pretty sure this wasn't it. But when we finally agreed that the script was finished, I couldn't deny the sense of loss I felt mixed in with the relief.

"Can you think of anyone who'd want to be in it?" Steve asked. He'd taken a fresh copy of the script and run it through the Xerox machine in the drama department office and, sitting on the back deck of Sigma Theta in our sweaters and coats, we were pleased with ourselves, reciting lines aloud to each other. Steve finished a can of Shlitz and threw it into the leafless hedge around the porch, then cracked another one.

His question took me a little from the side. "Aren't you using students from the drama program?"

He shook his head. "Can't. Those bastards are working on their own stage productions for the rest of the year. I already have you penciled in for the part of Alex," Steve said, that sly smile on his face. Alex, the brother who came out alive in the end, was the role I'd always cast myself in as we wrote. "You always read his lines differently," Steve said. "I could tell you liked that part."

The idea of acting in the movie was exciting. "Who else?" I said.

"Roscoe would do it. Jerome and Dan?"

"I think they'll all be game," Steve said. "The tricky part is going to be the girls."

I wanted to say Lucy's name, but stopped myself. Maybe I didn't want to admit how much I wanted her to be in the movie just so I could be around her, or maybe I was afraid of volunteering her for something she knew nothing about. But what I think, looking back on it now, is that it was the look Steve had given me when Lucy and I went into the closet that night in the abandoned mansion. That look that had been so full of things I couldn't entirely identify, but which had all told me one thing: Steve knew things about Lucy that I did not, and saying her name as we cast his movie would have been like trespassing on unknown and very private territory.

This was hardly the first time I'd thought my way through

this situation; after what had happened with Lucy in Coker's office, it had been impossible not to think about the possibilities for us. For me, that also meant thinking about what had gone on between her and Steve. It would have been ridiculous to believe they hadn't been involved, but who knew for how long, or how it had ended? Was it something that had happened Lucy's first year at Penton? What exactly *was* the nature of their relationship? I felt lost and frustrated.

Steve broke the silence, saying, "Sarah and Clara might be up for it. Mandy, too."

I nodded in agreement, but felt a nagging discontentment. For the past two weeks I'd worked day and night on the script, and the one thing I wanted, for Lucy to be involved, I didn't feel like I could safely bring up.

Hell, she could still be there, I thought. There were going to be lots of little jobs, and some big ones. Operating the camera, for instance. Who was going to do that if Steve and I were both acting in the film? When that issue came up, I'd mention Lucy's name, I decided; Steve was her friend, after all. He'd trust her with that. One way or another, I wanted Lucy there when we shot the movie.

When Steve and I finished pounding out a few more of the basic details, I pled exhaustion and headed back to the room for a shower and a nap.

***

Roscoe and I walked up to Sigma Theta that night together. The night was cold and arid, too dry for snow, and the cruel wind of an arctic front blowing down from Canada cut through our clothing like it wasn't even there. Halfway up to the hill, I felt a tap on my shoulder and looked over at Roscoe.

"Come here for a sec," he said, ducking behind the corner of Welch Hall. I joined him and immediately felt the wind's absence. It was almost as if we were standing inside a heated room.

I fumbled a cigarette from my pack and lit it, and we stood in the lee of the building, passing the butt back and forth. Roscoe was different from the kid I'd met at the beginning of the year. This new Roscoe was a little thinner, paler, more reserved. I'd thought for a time that whatever pain his father caused him had passed from him, had been cured somehow by the distance of being away from home, but that was stupid. He *was* different, changed in some vital, essential way. It wasn't that his last beating at the hands of his father had changed him, I thought. It was that *we* knew about it now. For a while he'd gotten to play a different character here at Penton, but now his old role had been thrust back on him, and he needed to figure out how to reconcile those parts of himself.

He caught me staring and said, "What?"

I shrugged. "Nothing. You look tired."

"Tired. Right." He dragged off the cigarette and handed it to me. "Nothing a beer or two won't cure."

"I don't think a simple beer or two is on the agenda for the evening, my friend."

"Really?" he said. "Meaning?"

"I don't know. Steve didn't go into it."

Roscoe said nothing for a few moments. Then, "You and Steve are tight lately."

"The script and all that."

He nodded and I smoked, then dropped the butt on the ground and crushed it out under my shoe.

***

The party at Sigma Theta lived up to the promise of Steve's secrecy. Its theme was Anything for Money, and the brothers had printed up special Sigma Theta cash just for the occasion. The objective was to earn as much of the money as possible by doing anything and everything people asked you to do. I took my wad of Sig Theta cash and tucked it in my pocket, then wished Roscoe good luck. I found myself pitying whatever poor girl encountered him first.

Wanting only to find a place to wait out the crowd, I angled and pushed through the sea of sweaty bodies in the cramped hallway. Music was pouring out of every open doorway, and the air reeked of pot and cigarette smoke and the musk of too many people crammed into a confined space. People yelled and waved money and barged from place to place, and only minutes after the start of the party, every inch of the house seemed to be filled with people engaged in acts I couldn't begin to fathom performing in public. Through one open door I saw a kneeling girl sucking Jack Daniels through a beer bong, her hands resting on the thighs of the brother holding the funnel above her head; in a corner of the hallway, a guy and a girl were lip-locked, her hand jammed down the front of his pants and moving; I saw a brother hand a chubby brunette a wad of cash as they walked into a room, then closed the door.

Steve's door stood open and nobody was inside, so I stepped in, closed the door behind me, and switched off his stereo, which had been blaring Led Zepplin. I was pulling a beer from his fridge when there was a loud knock on the door, which immediately opened. Jerome and Mandy backed into the room, arms around each other's necks. I saw her hand go to Jerome's crotch and he said, "That's right, baby," then saw me and stopped. "Hey, man. Didn't—"

I raised my hand to stop him and left the room, juked and squirmed through the throng of writhing bodies until I reached the living room, then tested the doorknob to the library. Unlocked. I cracked the door and peeked inside, saw no one there, then slipped into the room and locked the door behind me.

The Sig Theta library was really nothing more than a glorified study room. To validate its honorary title, someone had long ago populated the built-in bookshelves with a collection of classics.

Dickens, Twain, Dostoyevsky, Austen, Bronte, and the list went on. I reached out to pull a hardbound edition of *Bleak House* from the shelf, but was stopped by a rattling of the doorknob.

"Open up!" a voice yelled the other side of the door.

My hand suspended inches from the book, I tried to think of what to say.

The voice's owner pounded on the door, shaking it in the frame. "Open the fucking door! I gotta get in there!"

Unable to think of anything else to say, I yelled, "I'm having sex."

After a moment there was one last pound on the door, then nothing.

***

At around midnight, Lucy found me sitting outside on the front steps of the house. The party inside was still going strong, but as the participants had consumed increasingly massive quantities of alcohol and marijuana, the goings-on had deteriorated from mere crassness to a state that was numbing in its extremity.

Lucy sat down next to me and leaned over to nudge me with her shoulder. Before seeing her just then, I hadn't been aware that she was even at the party.

"How'd you do?" she said, raising her eyebrows at me.

I held out the wad of money Steve had handed me at the beginning of the party and nudged Lucy back. "Broke even. You?"

"Do you even need to ask?" She leaned back so she could slip her hand into the hip pocket of her jeans and pulled forth a thick wad of hundred dollar bills. I didn't know how much was there, but I *did* know that it was several times what we'd been given. It was by far the most money I'd seen anyone holding. I wondered what she'd done to earn the cash, and felt a stab of jealousy and realized I didn't want to think about it.

I said, "Nice," and then took a drag of my cigarette.

113

"You want it?" she asked.

Looking over at her, I saw the arch smile on her face and something inside me flipped and tightened. "What do you mean?"

"What's unclear? Do you want it?"

"Depends," I said, taking a sip of the beer I'd been nursing for so long that it had gone warm and flat. "That depends *entirely*."

Lucy studied me intently. "Ah, yes. The Puritan. I'd forgotten."

"Like I was saying, what do I have to do for it?"

She sat quietly for a moment, looking at me as if she was taking stock of something inside of my being. My mind ran through the list of possible scenarios she was devising in her head. I told myself that whatever it was, I wouldn't do it. Though she'd managed to manipulate me — and yes, that *was* what she'd done — into breaking into Sturges Hall and defiling Coker's office, I hadn't understood what I was doing at the time or why I was doing it. I knew now. A moment later I realized how full of shit I was. I'd do anything she asked.

But what she finally said was the very last thing I expected.

"Take me home with you for Thanksgiving break." She leaned away from me and looked briefly at my eyes, then down at the concrete between her boots.

I didn't know if I'd heard her correctly. Lucy came across as the most fearless person I'd ever known, the most audacious, and watching her now, head down, unable to meet my eyes, I realized she was scared. She was afraid I would say no to her.

For the second time in as many weeks, I found myself amazed and reeling at how *little* I really knew about the people in my life.

"Well, yeah," I fumbled out, hearing my words and wondering who was speaking them. "I'll call my parents. Sure."

"Are you just saying that to get my money?" The corners of her mouth just barely lifted.

I laughed. "Yup."

She slapped my arm. "Asshole." But she was smiling. Because of me, she was smiling. The feeling that grew inside of me was powerful and confused at the same time. In no way did I understand what had just happened, but I knew that this weekend I would call my mother and father and ask them if my friend Lucy could make the trip home with me for our five day break from school, and I knew that I would tell whatever lie needed to be told in order to convince them that the only correct answer to my question was "Yes, that sounds like a wonderful idea, Paul. By all means."

"Then here," Lucy said, folding her wad of bills into my hand. "This is yours." She kept her fingers closed on mine for a while, and suddenly all I wanted to do was hold her hand like that for as long as she'd let me. But then I thought of what was happening inside the house and about what she'd probably done for her money, and the feeling died.

I closed my hand around the money. "Thanks."

She shook her head and stood up. "No, Paul. Thank *you*."

And then she was gone, down the stairs, across the Hill, and out of sight around the corner of Phi Psi. I watched until I could no longer see her, then went inside to claim my prize.

CHAPTER SIXTEEN

A week before Thanksgiving I called and told my parents of my intention to bring Lucy home with me for break.

It was my mother who answered the phone that night, and when I told her about Lucy, she yelled to my father, "Paul's bringing a friend home for Thanksgiving. A girl!" The tone in her voice was unmistakable.

"It's not like that, Mom. She's just a friend." Even if I didn't have the slightest idea about the precise nature of our relationship, I did know that if we weren't exactly *friends*, we weren't really anything else, either. The prospect of spending five days alone at my house with Lucy and my parents was simultaneously exciting and terrifying to the point I felt nauseous; suddenly I wanted to be off the phone with my mother and up at the house with Steve and Roscoe, drinking a beer or ten.

"Um hmm," my mother responded in that same ironic, humored voice. "Well, it's fine either way. Bring whoever you want. Just make sure she understands the sleeping arrangements."

When I hung up with her, my first thought was to call Lucy, but I didn't know her number. Hell, I didn't even know where she lived. It hadn't occurred to me before, but now it seemed odd that Lucy would never have told me so much as what dorm she lived in. Yet another strange detail in our relationship.

I tossed the room for our student directory and found it at precisely the same moment I realized that I didn't know Lucy's last name. For a moment I considered paging through the entire thing, a catalogue of more than sixteen-hundred names and numbers, looking for junior girls named Lucy, but that felt all different kinds of wrong. Finally I decided that I would head up to the house and see if Jerome or Dan knew her last name. If that failed, I could always ask Steve. It was the last thing in the world I wanted to do, but I was going to have to track Lucy down eventually, and my options were limited.

***

As it turned out, neither Jerome nor Dan were at the house; they were both members of the Inter-Fraternal Council, the Greek governing body, and were attending a meeting at the student union. I stood for a moment outside of Dan's room and considered my options.

When a brother I recognized walked past, I asked if he knew where Steve was.

***

Steve, nude, was sitting in the middle of the tiled shower area on his floor of Sigma Theta in a blue plastic chair with metal legs. I recognized it as one of the chairs from the dining area in the basement. Several of the wall-mounted nozzles were pointed at him as he sat in a converging hurricane of water, drinking a beer. A plastic cooler full of ice and bottles rested on the floor at his side. Steam filled the room, and I couldn't see the corners, which was vaguely unnerving. Almost immediately I began to sweat.

"Paul," he said, "come on in." It wasn't unusual for Sigma Theta brothers to gather in the shower, strip naked, and sit for hours in a cluster drinking beer and smoking cigarettes, every one of the showerheads spraying hot water, the windows wide open for ventilation, even in the heart of winter. Living in a fraternity

117

house seemed to have some effect on one's level of comfort with public nudity. I couldn't get used to it.

"No thanks," I answered, unsure where to look. Finally I settled on the eyes, noting Steve's humored look as I did so. "I just have a question for you, actually."

"All right," he said, tipping beer back. "Shoot."

"It's just that—," I started, then stalled. "I was wondering if you knew Lucy's last name or phone number, or where she lives."

His hazy, steam-obscured face underwent a strange sequence of changes. I realized he probably knew nothing about the things Lucy and I had done together, and that if he did, he probably wouldn't like it. "Lucy," he finally said. "What for?"

"She asked me to call her," I lied. Suddenly I wanted very much to be gone from the shower room, from the house; hell, from the campus.

"You want her number?" Steve asked. "Tell me, Paul. Why do you *really* want her number, bro?"

"I—" I what? What had I wandered into here? It felt like there had to be some kind of way out of this, some direction where the ground wouldn't fall off beneath my feet, but then I realized that direction may very well have been *back*. But it was too late for that now. I'd put myself here knowing full well how it could play out, and now all I could do was trust that everything would shake out in the end. There was no other way to go.

Hell with it, I thought. "She's supposed to come home with me over break. I just talked to my folks and they said it was okay, so I need to get in touch with her and let her know."

"Home with you," Steve said.

"That's right. For Thanksgiving."

"Why?"

"I don't know. She didn't say. She only said that she wanted to come with me."

"Home," he said. "With you." As though trying to convince himself he'd heard the words correctly.

"Right."

Steve looked down at the bottle in his hand, and for a crazy moment I was sure he would chuck it at me, maybe at my head, anywhere vital. Then he looked back up, his expression flat. "Three six eight four," he said. "Her extension."

He leaned back into the apex of the spray. The heat in the room was fantastic.

"Thanks," I said, feeling small. "Look, Steve, I don't know if—"

But Steve held up a hand to stop me. "Don't," he said. "Just go."

So I went, my tail between my legs.

CHAPTER SEVENTEEN

That Tuesday after my last class, I headed back to Smith to pack a bag for the trip. The original plan had been for my parents to buy me a plane ticket, but Lucy insisted that we drive. She had a car on campus. Her last class got out at three, she said, and she would swing by my dorm to pick me up no later than three fifteen. That gave me about half an hour to get ready.

When I got back to the room, Roscoe was gone, though before he left he'd managed to clean up his half of the room to the point it no longer looked like someone had tossed it for valuables. As time for break had approached his mood had darkened, and I knew he was thinking about having to spend the holiday with his father. Most of his class work had gone undone, and his hygiene had suffered; I didn't think he had changed his jeans in the last week.

He'd left a sheet of notebook paper draped over my typewriter.

Paco, the note said in Roscoe's familiar scrawl, *do me a favor and get some play while you're home with Lucy. I can't stand living with a fucking virgin anymore. Everyone laughs at me when I tell them you've never gotten any. Just be considerate, bro. Do it for me if not for yourself.*

-Roscoe Ballantemps (your friend).

Smiling to myself, I dropped the note back on the desk, then hauled my gray duffel out from under the bunk and stuffed it full of my warmest clothing. Though it was chilly in Ohio, the late November weather in Philly could be brutal. I packed a couple of books for my Intro to English class and my Psych text, knowing that there was little hope of getting any reading done, but going through the motions anyway. Some things in this life you just have to do for the peace of mind. I grabbed my bag, locked the room, and headed downstairs to wait.

***

I don't know what I'd expected to see Lucy pull up in, but the nifty little Mercedes coup she guided to the curb definitely hadn't been one of the possibilities I'd considered.

She popped the trunk and I loaded my stuff, then hopped into the passenger side seat. The car looked attractive and well-maintained from the outside, the maroon paint sparking, hardly a trace of mud anywhere, even on the wheels. On the inside, however, chaos ruled. Clothes, wrappers, and empty cans of soda and beer covered almost every inch of floor space, and while the seats weren't exactly *filthy*, they certainly defied categorization as clean. I felt like I'd learned something, though I didn't know what it was.

"Ready?" Lucy asked. She seemed distracted, a little harried, but she looked beautiful. Her hair was pulled back in way I'd never seen her wear it, fixed at the back with a claw-like barrette. The instant I sat down in the car I could smell her perfume, flowery and light, the furthest thing from overpowering, but impossible to miss.

I said, "Nice car. Yours?"

"Graduation present from high school. You'll have to excuse the mess. Not much time to clean lately."

"No problem," I said. I pulled forth a small, black rock that

121

had been digging into my left hip. "No problem at all."

"Good," she said. "Then let's get the fuck out of Dodge."

***

We drove straight through the waning afternoon and into the night, stopping only when one of us desperately needed to use the bathroom, or when the gas tank was teetering on the edge of empty.

The night before, I'd made up my mind to try to learn more about Lucy. Though we'd had several long conversations in the past, she'd always avoided sharing personal details about herself. Not in my wildest dreams did I fancy myself a perceptive person, but a baboon would have noticed the care she took to steer conversation away from herself.

So I decided to try.

The first questions were simple enough, and I let long silences hang between them, not wanting Lucy to feel as though I was prying. I started with the car. An innocent enough lead-in, I thought. We were, after all, *in* the car. Made sense to me.

"This your dad's old car?"

"No," she replied. "New off the lot when I got it."

"Did you get to pick it out?"

"No." And then five minutes of silence, the only sounds the whipping of wind from outside and the occasional *buh-bump* as the car crossed an uneven section of road. I tried a new approach.

"Where does your family live?"

She propped her left elbow on the window-frame, rested her chin on her hand, and stared straight ahead at the road, brow furled. After some time, she said, "A town called Danbury. Near Cincinnati."

"I didn't know you were from Ohio."

"It never came up."

I thought about saying something else, but then the time had gone and all I could do was sit in the uncomfortable silence and wonder how long I would have to wait before I could try again, and if all of break would be like this.

***

We left Ohio and entered Pennsylvania. I told Lucy that I'd be happy to drive for a while when we stopped for gas. She shrugged and climbed into the passenger-side seat. She sat with her head turned away from me, and I wondered what she was thinking. That she'd made a terrible mistake asking to come home with me? That I was nosey and annoying? I started the car up and pulled back onto I-70, wondering if there was any way to pull her away from her deep consideration of oncoming traffic and cattle fields and back into the car with me.

In the end, I decided to do nothing.

We moved through western and central Pennsylvania without stopping once, passing Pittsburgh, New Stanton, Washington, and any number of other small burgs too insignificant to warrant signage. Finally, we started seeing signs for Harrisburg, and I knew that we only had two hours to go. By that point, what had seemed like a welcome opportunity to get to know Lucy had turned into a sour experience, and I was more than a little anxious to be out of the car.

A little under two hours later, I heard myself say, "Ah," as a green, underlit sign for the Pennsylvania Turnpike whipped past.

Lucy looked over at me, the first time she'd acknowledged my presence in more than an hour. "What?"

"Almost there."

"Good. I don't know how much more of this my ass can take."

Apparently her emotional weather had shifted. She was no longer staring out her window; rather, she was looking back at me, an almost girlishly excited look on her face.

I felt I should say something in way of a response to stop her

123

from going away again. I said, "When I stand up, all the blood's going to rush from my ass to my head and I'm going to face-plant."

She laughed and brushed my arm, and we broke into the kind of nonsensical banter that means nothing, most of which was punctuated by bursts of her laughter, which was alternately gruff and musical, depending on what she was responding to. I told her about my first day at Penton, walking into the room and finding Roscoe hard at work. She came back with a story about her freshman year roommate, a tiny girl from California who had looked nothing if not pure and innocent, but who was anything but. Over the course of the year, Lucy said, she'd carved nearly fifty notches in her sorority paddle.

"I don't know where she got the energy," Lucy said, laughing uncontrollably. "Three nights a week I'd go to bed at midnight and then wake up when she and whatever frat boy she'd brought home barged in. And it's not like that was just the first couple of weeks of school. That was the whole *year*. It was amazing."

I loved hearing her laugh, and as we talked more and more I knew this was what I wanted. To be with Lucy, like this. I thought that I would go to great lengths to keep her happy like this, and I knew I could.

By this time it was a little after midnight, and my eyes were bleary from looking at the nighttime road for the last six hours. I tried to keep my focus on the road, but my mind began to wander, and I found myself thinking about my childhood here, and how my house and town would look to Lucy. To be sure, the town was anything but bustling. Boring would be a better word.

"Is this it?" Lucy asked as we entered Swarthmore, passing the library, then Park Avenue Pizza, where I used to meet my friends before heading out for a movie or a dance. This late at night the pizzeria was closed, but I felt comfort just seeing it there, like always. We passed the travel agency where my mother had worked for a time before I was born, and then the commuter train station.

It was just as I'd left it.

As I grew older, my parents regretted that there weren't more things to *do* in Swarthmore...that it was too bland and boring for a kid my age, but I never agreed with them. For me, the town and the woods and the school had been perfect. Sure, I'd been sheltered from some of the things other of my friends who lived in nearby towns had gotten into, but in my mind that was what college was for. I loved it here. The reluctance I'd felt about leaving Penton and coming home dissipated, and I realized how excited I was to be back home.

I took the winding route through Swarthmore College instead of going around, which would have been faster. A few students wandered around here and there. Like us, they were on break for Thanksgiving and the campus was empty and quiet. From the passenger's seat, Lucy took it all in—the field house and tennis courts, the Sharples clocktower, sprawling Parrish Hall, which presided over the sloping grass commons between the college and the town—gazing intently though her window, wistful again. We were no more than a quarter-mile from my house when she said something I couldn't hear.

"What?" I asked, braking to a stop in front of Hicks Hall, the engineering building. My house was only a couple of blocks away now, and I felt energized at the prospect of being there.

Though she didn't look at me, she repeated herself, and this time I heard the words just fine.

"I said, this must have been a wonderful place to be a kid."

"It was," I answered, speaking more to myself than to her.

CHAPTER EIGHTEEN

During the spring and summer, the façade of our blocky brick house was covered with ivy all the way from the ground to the flat, tar-sealed roof that my father was always patching and leveling. Each winter the ivy died, and when it made its return the next year, the appearance of the house changed, taking on a warm and lived-in look. The last time I'd seen the house had been in August, and I'd assumed the ivy would still be there, that the house would be the same as it had been when I left. That it wasn't seemed unnatural to me. What else had I missed?

I reached for the ignition, but Lucy's hand settled on my wrist. I looked over at her and saw that her eyes were full of tears.

"Hey, what's wrong?" I said, turning my hand over and closing it around hers.

"I just want you to know—" Her voice broke and she looked down at our hands for a moment before trying again. When she brought her eyes back up to look at me, her own features were so full of anxiety that I could barely stand to look at her face. "I know I can be difficult sometimes," she said. "And I know I can act crazy, and that you've probably heard things about me and what I've done. But I wanted you to know that I won't cause problems between you and your parents. Okay? I *won't*."

"You couldn't if you tried," I said. "My parents are ridiculously understanding."

Lucy smiled, but the anxiety hadn't left her eyes. "I just wanted to tell you that. I'm ready now."

We got out of the car, took our bags from the trunk, and headed for the door.

***

My father was still awake, despite the late hour. Before we even reached the door he came outside to greet us, wearing flannel pajama bottoms, a white knit sweater, and his old wool-lined slippers. His graying hair stuck up at crazy angles, and I knew he'd dozed off for a while in front of the TV, probably with his feet up on the ottoman and a gin and tonic propped between his legs. His feet crunched over the thin layer of snow and ice that coated the driveway as he approached us, his breath vaporous in the cold night.

He hugged me and clapped me on the back, then let me go and stepped back, holding me by the shoulders at arm's length.

"Goddamnit," he finally said, "you've been into the beer, haven't you?"

I smiled and shrugged. "I'll plead the fifth on that one, Dad."

"No, I can *see* it. When you left here you were all skin and bones. Now you have a belly you could rest a plate on."

"Come on, it's not that bad."

He laughed. "No, it's not, but it *will* be if you're not careful." He swatted me on the arm, still chuckling. "Who knew the day would come? Now introduce me to your friend."

***

My mother was asleep, but she'd fixed the beds with fresh sheets, both in my room and in the guest room, which was — and I'm sure this had irritated my mother to no end — right next to my room. Lucy and I carried our bags upstairs and dropped them in our respective rooms. When we went back downstairs, my father was in the kitchen, rinsing his glass out in the sink and smoking a cigarette.

"You guys must be bushed," he said, crushing his cigarette out. The ashtray he used this time I'd made for him in the fifth grade. It was a ceramic turtle with the top of its shell hollowed out into a dish.

In actuality, I wasn't tired in the least. Long drives left me feeling hyper and a little loose in the head, and I knew that if I tried to go to sleep right now I'd lie there tossing and turning for hours. Plus, watching my dad smoke, now *I* wanted a cigarette.

"But," my dad continued, "if you need to unwind first, I bought you some beer. It's in the downstairs fridge. Imported. Hope you don't mind. I know how you college kids like that cheap crap."

"Jeez, you didn't have to do that, Dad."

"I wanted to. Oh, and if you're going to smoke, make sure you do it down there. Your mother would faint if she saw you, and I'd never hear the end of it."

"How did you — ?"

He waved the question off. "Kiddo, next time you want to hide that you smoke from someone, don't go walking around with a pack of Camels sticking out of your breast pocket."

I looked down. "Oh."

"Oh, indeed," he said, then gave me a wink.

My father said goodnight, and then Lucy and I walked down the squeaky wooden stairs to the basement. The carpeting was a bright enough red to make your head hurt. We went to the laundry room and I took two Heinekens from the refrigerator, lit our cigarettes, and wordlessly, we sat on the couch that fronted the TV.

"Thank god for nicotine," I said, breathing out a pale plume of smoke.

"I like your dad," Lucy said. "He seems like a nice man. I

128

can't wait to meet your mom."

"You won't have to wait long," I said. "If she lets us sleep past seven tomorrow morning it'll be a miracle." I took a sip of beer and liked the taste. I took another, longer swallow. "Damn, that's pretty good."

Lucy took a drink. "It is."

"You know," I said, looking at the floor, "my parents are going to assume we're together." It was a topic I'd been waiting to bring up, but it had never seemed like the right time. Now that I'd actually said the words, I felt presumptuous and embarrassed.

"Does that bother you?"

"Bother me? No...I mean, no. Why would it—?"

Lucy put her hand on mine and laughed. "Whoa, Paul. It's fine. I don't mind if they think we're together. That's fine. Is that okay with you?"

"Yeah," I said. "It's okay with me." I squeezed her hand and sat back on the couch, feeling exhilarated.

We finished our beers, and after taking the bottles into the laundry room, we made our way upstairs. From inside my parents' bedroom I could hear my dad's steady, low snore, a sound that was strangely reassuring.

At the door to Lucy's room, I said, "Sleep well."

She opened her door and then turned back to me. "This is so much better than going back to my own house. Thank you." She rose up on her tip-toes and planted a light kiss on my lips, and then she stepped into her bedroom and closed the door softly behind her.

For a very long while I stood there, eyes closed, until I finally realized I was holding my breath and let it go. And all I could think was that after everything that had happened between us, she had finally kissed me. I wondered what she was in her room thinking, if she knew I was still standing outside her door, and that was enough to get me moving.

CHAPTER NINETEEN

The majority of my most vivid memories are marked at the beginning by waking up. Maybe this is because my mind has been conditioned through my work at the magazine by the basic dramatic structure of three acts…beginning, middle, end. Or maybe it's because my strongest impressions are made during that liminal time between sleep and awareness. I've heard the imagination is at its most potent level then; maybe the same goes for memory. I don't know, and maybe it doesn't matter. Anyway, the important thing is my memory of that first day home with Lucy began with waking.

My eyes opened when two sensory messages arrived at my brain more or less simultaneously; the smell of bacon cooking, and the sound of voices.

I sat up, listening more carefully. One of the voices was Lucy's, the other my mother's. *Oh god*, I thought, but then I heard Lucy's voice and my mother's laughter, loud and unfettered. Curious and a little apprehensive, I put on the red and green terry cloth robe I'd been wearing since I was fifteen and went downstairs.

"Ah," my mother said when I walked into the kitchen, looking, I'm sure, like death. "It emerges from its lair."

"Mmm," I said, rubbing at my eyes. "Hi, Mom."

"Come over here," she said, holding her arms out. "Your father says you're fat."

I went to her and gave her a hug. Over her shoulder, I saw Lucy sitting at the kitchen table, smiling at us. She looked tired, but relaxed. I wondered how much she'd slept.

"So, Lucy and I have been talking," my mother said, raising her eyebrows at me, then turned to favor Lucy with a conspiratorial look.

"Wow," I said. "That's really something. Talking. About what?" All I wanted was a cup of coffee.

My mother saw me looking around and said, "The machine broke, so we've been using the percolator. Over there." She nodded at the stove. I took a mug from the cabinet and poured myself some.

Then Lucy answered the question I'd asked my mother. "About how long we've been together, how we met. You know, that kind of stuff."

"Been together?" I said, turning to face her.

"Mm hmm."

"And," I said, "what did you tell her?" I was very aware of the fact that my mother was looking at me. I remembered the conversation I'd had with her a couple of weeks ago where I'd insisted that Lucy and I were just friends.

"That we met early in the year at the student union, and that you're the sweetest guy on the face of the earth. That kind of thing. She *was* curious about why you never told her about us."

"About *us*."

My mother laughed and I could tell she thought I had been ashamed or afraid to tell her I was dating someone, or maybe just to tell her I was dating someone other than Jo. I felt like an idiot and pressed my eyes shut, wishing I was back in my bed.

"Seriously, Paul, why would you hide this darling creature?"

I thought about how to answer, but couldn't think of anything that wouldn't sound like a clumsy lie. Instead, I just shook my head and said, "Jesus."

***

All of the relatives who lived in a fifty-mile radius were coming over for Thanksgiving dinner, and my mother was nearly overwhelmed with all the details of planning dinner. After breakfast, Lucy and I offered to go to the store for her.

In the car, Lucy read the list. "Turkey Hill vanilla ice cream, six cloves of garlic, black peppercorns, and two pounds of Wawa coffee." After reading the last item, she glanced over at me. "Wawa?"

"My mom won't drink any other kind." I returned her gaze. "And speaking of my mother."

She shrugged. "I guess I just told her what I wanted to be true."

"What you wanted…. Wait, are you saying that you want to be *with* me? Like, my girlfriend or something?" As soon as I said the words I wanted to take them back, aware of how immature I must sound to her. We'd had the conversation last night about my parents assuming we were an item, but I thought that was that. Now I was lost.

"Something like that, maybe."

"Look," I said. "I'm not trying to be dense, but do you really like me? Like, *like me* like me?"

She laughed and said, "That's four 'likes,' Paul."

"Sorry. I just don't know what to say. I feel like a moron. I'm sorry." I wanted to say that I was sorry again, but I'd already said it twice. And there went another "like." Good Lord. For a moment I thought about opening the car door and bailing out onto MacDade Boulevard.

"It's okay," she said.

"I—"

Lucy held up her hand. "We'll figure it out. For now, let's just

132

go to the store. But for what it's worth, I really *did* mean what I told your mom."

Considering the stupid smile I couldn't get off my face, I wouldn't have blamed the cashier at Wawa for thinking I was simple-minded.

***

When we got back, my mother put all of us to work in the kitchen. The turkey went in the oven at ten so that it would be done for dinner at five. I skinned potatoes and then passed them on to Lucy, who quartered them and dropped them in a bowl of water that would be stored in the fridge until later. We sliced apples for pie, then cleaned the good silver and china and set the table.

My last chore was to make the green bean casserole, which I'd been doing every year since I was old enough to take my mom's directions. Lucy and I worked as a team; I washed the green beans and she chopped the ends off, then split the beans down the middle. We boiled the beans and then left them in a Tupperware bowl to cool until later, when I would mix them with cream of mushroom soup and French fried onions. All the while I kept sneaking glances at Lucy, wondering if I had to keep *sneaking* them at all.

My mom walked into the kitchen, a list in her hand. "That's it," she said. "Go do something with Lucy. Go on, go." Since there wasn't really much to do, I thought it would be nice to take a walk around the college.

It was cold, but not bitterly so, and walking kept us warm enough inside our coats. I kept looking over at Lucy and smiling, wondering if I'd ever know the right thing to say again. As we entered the college, Lucy slipped her arm through mine and leaned into me. When we passed by the edge of the Crum woods that abutted the college's lacrosse field, Lucy pointed over at a trail that sloped down into the trees just past the DuPont math

133

building.

"Can we take a look?"

Shrugging, I said, "The trails might not be in such good shape. They get pretty rough in the winter."

"We'll be careful," she said, and headed toward the trees.

Just into the heart of the woods the trail forked, one of the branches heading off down toward the creek, the other winding its way along the edge of the college. We took the latter, which was fraught with icy spots and protruding rocks. After a few minutes, Lucy grabbed my arm to stop me.

"Look," she said, resting her hand on the trunk of an old birch tree, the first twenty feet of which was inlaid with carved initials. Some of them I'd been looking at since I was a kid, and had watched as they slowly rose with the growth of the tree. The more recent engravings were lighter, less permanent looking.

"Are you up here?" she asked.

"Are you kidding?" I laughed.

"Give me your keys."

I reached into my coat pocket and gave her the key ring. I always carried a Swiss Army knife with my keys, and Lucy opened the nail file and set to work on the tree. I slipped a cigarette out of my pocket and sat down on a fallen tree to watch as she worked. Above us I heard a car pull into the parking lot of Lang Hall, the faint sound of voices talking and laughing. Small animals rattled around in the underbrush. Far below I could hear the sound of the Crum Creek gurgling over the rocks by the trestle. They were all the sounds of home, and I realized suddenly that I felt good and comfortable.

After a few minutes, Lucy stepped back to look at her work.

"There. Not bad."

Into the smooth gray bark of the tree, she'd carved, PAUL + LUCY. The words were contained by the outline of a heart. The confusion I'd been feeling all day — ever since Lucy had asked if she could come home with me, really—doubled.

"What do you think?" she said.

I stood and walked to her and put my arms around her from behind, feeling clumsy, not quite sure it was okay but feeling bold enough to try. "It's nice."

"Yeah," she said. "It is." Then she turned to face me and put her arms around my neck and I kissed her, feeling at first like someone trying to will himself into a dream, then feeling nothing but warm.

CHAPTER TWENTY

Thanksgiving dinner was euphoric. All night I kept catching Lucy's eyes across the table, and each time it happened, I felt electrified.

Lucy was wonderful with the rest of my family. She charmed my aunt Anne and uncle Larry, talking knowledgeably about art and books, played with their two young children, looking as comfortable bouncing them on her knee as she did everything else. She helped me and my mother serve dinner, filled glasses of wine when they were empty, ate with delicate and impeccable manners. I would never have described my own family as genteel, but having observed the table manners of some of the Sigma Theta brothers, I knew we were more refined than many families. Lucy had obviously been raised in a similar environment, and though her table manners unto themselves told me little about her, I realized that I had learned something valuable.

When we finally finished eating and drinking, and when my father and I had cleared the table and scraped the plates clean, my aunt and uncle left to drive the short distance home to Media.

"Sleepy," my dad said, teetering a little. He'd started with a beer or two as we cooked, moved on to his scotch during dinner, and then, as he ate apple pie with vanilla ice cream, had soldiered his way through a couple of glasses of the sweet Muscat my mother liked so much. His drunkenness showed itself only in the slightly unsteady way he moved.

"Paul and I can clean up," Lucy said, smiling at him. "Go to bed."

"No," my dad said. "I can help." But a minute later I heard him stomping up the stairs toward the bedroom. We found my mother asleep in my dad's recliner, her bare feet propped up on the footrest.

"Poor thing," Lucy whispered. "Should we wake her up, get her upstairs?"

I shook my head and took the light blanket that was draped over the back of the sofa, shook it open, and laid it gently over her.

"Mmm, thanks," she said, her voice muzzy with sleep, and then she was gone again, her hands wrapped in the soft cotton of the blanket.

Lucy and I went back to the kitchen and, as quietly as we could, washed and dried the dishes in conveyor-belt fashion. I couldn't stop thinking about what had happened in the woods and wanted to kiss her again, but didn't know how to do it. What was I to her? It was the thing I wanted to know most, and the thing I was most afraid to ask. Lucy had already demonstrated how quickly her mood could change, and I didn't want to risk ruining the good time she seemed to be having.

By the time we were finished cleaning up, my hands were pruned, and my lower back hurt from standing over the sink for so long. We wiped the dining room table clean, wrapped the leftovers, and took the trash out. Done with all of that, we went out onto the back patio to smoke and finish the last of the Muscat. We sat in the Adirondack chairs and Lucy spread a blanket over her legs.

"So," I said, "what do you think?"

"Of what?"

"My family, what else?"

She took a drag from her cigarette, then said, "I don't think I even have the words to answer that question, Paul. My family...."

I was silent.

"I've never been around a family like yours," she said.

I nodded. "They're pretty great."

"Not just them," she said. "You, too." She thought for a moment, and then added, "These have been two great days, the best I can remember having in forever."

Her words aroused so many questions in my head, things I'd wondered since the first time we'd met at the old house in Penton. Questions about her own family. Questions about her past. Why she did the things she did.

Almost as if she could read my thoughts, she turned to me and said, "I know I haven't told you much about myself. Thank you for not asking."

"It's okay," I said. "I guess you'll tell me when you're ready."

"Someday soon," she said. We crushed out our cigarettes and went inside.

***

Sometime later, I jolted awake. There was a wedge of yellow light from the hallway cast across the carpet, and then the door eased closed and it was gone.

Then I heard Lucy's voice.

"It's me," she whispered from somewhere close. My eyes had adjusted enough that I could see a faint outline of her body silhouetted against the dark.

"Are you okay?" I asked, propping myself on an elbow.

"I need you to hold me," she said.

"Okay. Come here," I whispered, moving to the far side of the bed. Still half asleep, I was nonetheless scared that my parents might find Lucy and me together in my room.

As she passed the window, the moon lit one side of her face for a moment, and then she was standing beside the bed. She pulled her nightgown up and over her head, then dropped it to the floor.

A moment of the purest panic constricted every cell in my body, shivering my scalp, tightening the skin of my arms and stomach, the small of my back. I trembled and felt nauseated. *Wait*, I almost said, *wait not here no we can't I can't do this*. But I didn't say any of those things, and then she lay down facing me and I felt her hands on my skin, first on my chest, then moving softly over my ribs and across my back, and everywhere her fingers went I felt cool electricity. My entire body jerked when she touched my stomach.

"Sorry," I whispered, and my voice was shaking. The muscles in my stomach and groin danced as though a current ran through them.

"It's okay," Lucy said, and took my hand in hers and draped my arm over her. "Here."

The feel of her warm skin under my hand shocked me. We moved closer and her breasts pressed against me, and her leg slid over mine. I felt her nipples hard against my chest. I ran my fingers down her back and over the smooth skin of her butt, heard the catch of her breath in my ear. She kissed my neck, the underside of my jaw, moved to my mouth. Everywhere she went, she left cool moisture.

"Lie back," she said. I did and she pulled my boxer shorts off, then moved her way up my body and straddled me, leaned down, and kissed me.

"Have you done this before?" she whispered.

"No," I said, barely able to draw a breath. I rested my hands on her hips but my fingers twitched. Above me Lucy was a dark shape, then she leaned down and looked into my eyes. Hers were black, and I felt her warm breath on my mouth and chin.

"Do you want this?" she asked, then kissed my throat.

I tried to say something, but my throat was dry and clicked. I nodded.

She shifted on top of me and I felt a warm wetness, and then I was inside of her, all the way, and she held me there.

"Tell me when you're close," she said, then began to move and soon I was moving with her. She made small noises as she rocked her hips.

All too soon I felt myself tightening, a shiver in my brain. "Lucy, I—"

She stopped and leaned forward and I came out of her, felt the cool air on me. Her breasts grazed my mouth and I took a nipple into my mouth and kissed it, ran my tongue around it. Lucy inhaled sharply.

"Are you okay now?" she whispered into my ear.

"I think so," I said.

She reached between us and guided me, sat back, and ground her pelvis into mine, back and forth, back and forth. The pressure was maddening and I could feel my control slipping, started to pull myself out of her again. I didn't want for it to be over, not so quickly.

"Stay," she whispered, and leaned into my chest, kissing my neck.

Moments later, face buried in the hollow of her neck and shoulder, I made a sound and came, heard her saying something as she stroked the skin of my arms and chest. Afterwards I stayed there, shaking, thinking everything and nothing all at once.

***

When I woke in the morning she had gone back to her room. I put my head back on the pillow and fell asleep again.

CHAPTER TWENTY-ONE

Half an hour after I finally got out of bed and wandered downstairs, I had almost managed to convince myself that last night had really happened. There were small red marks on my neck and one on my cheek. Before coming downstairs I'd stripped the bed and stuffed the sheet into the hamper, just in case.

My mother and father had left a note for us on the kitchen counter. They were off at a post-Thanksgiving sale at Sears and would be back around lunch. There were still plenty of leftovers if we wanted something to nibble on.

And then Lucy walked into the kitchen wearing sweatpants and a T-shirt, and she kissed me on the mouth and said, "Well, good morning," and I *knew* it had happened. "I'm hungry," she said as she sat down at the counter with a mug of coffee. She propped a bare foot on my knee and I stroked it. "Can we eat somewhere?"

"Yeah. Why don't we walk downtown? It's a little late for breakfast and a little early for lunch, but...."

She leaned forward on her stool and put her hands on either side of my face. "Are you okay with last night?" she whispered.

"Yeah," I said. "Sorry. I was babbling, wasn't I?"

"Starting to. I just wanted to make sure everything was all

141

right between us."

I smiled and ran my hand up her calf. "Can I ask you something?"

"What?"

"Does this mean that I can kiss you now if I get the urge?"

"Is this an urge you're having presently?"

"Well, yeah."

"Then come here."

***

We walked through the Swarthmore College campus and into town, talking and smoking. Not much was open the day after Thanksgiving, but Park Avenue Pizza was serving, so we went inside and took an open booth in the front of the restaurant, near the window.

When I looked up from the menu, there was Jo, just a few booths away. She looked older, and for a second I wasn't even sure it was her. Since I'd known her Jo had worn her hair long and free, but now it was cut short and pulled back away from her face. As I watched, she leaned into the guy sitting next to her and laughed, brushing his chest with her hand, and when she looked back down, her eyes caught my own and her smile faltered for a moment.

I felt a shock go through my body and fought the urge to look away. Inside of me thoughts of what I'd done last night with Lucy mixed with a kind of jealousy for the guy Jo was with. I smiled the best I could and raised my hand in what started out to be a wave but fell short. Lucy swiveled in her seat to look, then back.

"Friend?" she said.

"Yeah, kind of."

"Do you want to go over and say hi?"

I shook my head. "I don't think we have anything to say."

She shrugged. "Okay."

When Jo left a few minutes later, she smiled as she passed

142

and said, "Hi, Paul," and then she was gone and I could breathe again.

***

Early the next morning we loaded our stuff into Lucy's car, hugged and kissed my mother and father goodbye, and set off for Ohio.

CHAPTER TWENTY-TWO

No relationship in my life has ever rivaled the obsessive power of the time I was involved with Lucy. In a distant and unacknowledged sort of way, I'd always understood that you only get to have that kind of love once. Even if my marriage to Dottie is more substantial and spans decades, it is a candle in the wake of a star.

In a very real way, my love for Lucy defined the way I was going to be for the rest of my life. In its confines I discovered who I was. Or it *made* me who I was, for better or worse. At times I wished I had never known Lucy, that I had chosen to stay home that first night Roscoe asked me to come out with him, when we ended up at the old mansion. At other times, I got lost speculating about how my life would be if Lucy were still alive. Those were the darkest times.

After her death there had been other women, of course, women before Dottie. One by one I drove them away. I'd seen friends do the same thing to women, but they never seemed aware of what they were doing. I knew. But if I didn't want to be *with* anyone, I didn't want to be alone, either. So I'd keep things going until something inside of me said it was time, then end it.

When I look back on those days I don't feel guilt. I can't blame myself for something I couldn't control; I was too young and too damaged to help myself. But if I had been a doctor in charge of my own care, I would have locked myself away from people for a good long time. There was a calm, vicious monster inside me. During that period of my life I believe I was a dangerous man, maybe a worse kind of dangerous than the men who couldn't *hide* what they were. I could; I was great at it. Women had no way of knowing what was coming their way until it was upon them, and I know I hurt one or two of them badly.

There was one in particular, a girl named Ashley, who I met at a law office where I was doing secretarial work after graduating from Penton. She was tall and slender and wore square-ish librarian glasses that slipped down her nose when she smiled. We dated for a number of months, ate dinner at dozens of restaurants around Columbus, saw a play or two in small local theaters, hiked in the Olentangy nature preserve, went to bed any chance we got. On my birthday she told me she loved me, and the next day I told her we were through. It was brutal and final, and I felt nothing when I did it.

I sometimes wonder what became of Ashley and the rest of those girls, and when I catch myself doing so I end those episodes with the same self-admonishment, that I was giving myself too much credit, making myself more important to them than I had been. But I don't know. I hope am I right.

After Lucy died I simply lost access to my soul. Once I got out of the hospital I continued on as though nothing had ever happened, this despite the insistence of the hospital counselor that I had to face Lucy's death on a day-to-day basis. I nodded and assured him I knew that was true, but I'd already chosen another path.

I woke every morning, my hands still wrapped in bandages that soaked through sometimes with dark yellow pus, and told myself that none of it was very important. There had been an accident; it wasn't my fault; I had to move on. The same kinds of things happened to people all the time.

My mother and father had come to Ohio to stay with me in the hospital, and they both wanted me to come home for a while. I should have. Maybe being with them, being surrounded by their love, would have allowed me to heal. Instead, I stayed in Penton and went back to class as quickly as possible.

I'd been told Roscoe wouldn't be back. Eventually I would reestablish contact with him, but only once he and I were ready. The college decided not to give me a new roommate, and I was thankful. Most nights I spent in my room alone, reading or writing, doing anything but letting my brain lay idle.

Like mine, Steve's injuries had been superficial ones, nothing he wouldn't recover from in time, but in his eyes I always saw the fire. The first time I saw him outside of the hospital, I was on my way to class. He was walking between Jerome and Dan on the other side of Spring Street, and I could tell they were trying to get him to laugh, to talk, something. But he walked with his head down, watching his feet move. Feeling guilty and slimy, like a fraud, I put my head down, too, and pretended I hadn't seen them. We were almost clear of each other when I heard Dan's voice.

"Hey, Paul!"

I stopped and turned and faced them across the street. "Hi," I said, and waved. "How's it going?" I stepped onto the grass to get out of the way of the other students on their way to wherever.

Steve hadn't looked at me yet, and I knew immediately that he had been walking with his head down because he had seen me, too. It was a sickening realization.

"Come up to the house later," Dan called out, apparently sensing Steve's discomfort. "Have a beer."

"Okay," I said, knowing I would do no such thing. "Later." And then they rejoined the flow of students heading back toward the dorms. I watched them until they crossed Winter Street and disappeared behind Welch Hall, my chest heavy with the first true grief I'd felt since my days in the hospital. I had lost Lucy, yes, but she was only the most obvious casualty of the fire. I felt the acute emptiness of knowing that I was going to have to start all over again.

For Steve, as for me, it would be that night for a very long time, but I couldn't be there with him. While we were both trapped there, we were trapped alone; I didn't want to let him share my isolation and anger any more than he wanted me to share his. So I figured out where he would be at what time and made sure to be elsewhere. Even as I was doing these things, I felt a certain level of disgust at my own actions, but I was powerless to stop a process that had already spiraled well out of my control.

Even when I met Dottie several years after college, I was still incapable of being honest with her or myself. Standing outside on the porch of my apartment in Columbus, Dottie had asked me where I'd gotten the scars on my hands.

"In a fire," I told her. "When I was in college." This is what I always told people when they asked, and usually that was enough, an answer that, by omission, told the listener there was nothing else to hear. At least, nothing I was willing to say.

She winced, and I felt the familiar twinge of unease behind my eyes. "God, what happened?"

We'd had a pleasant evening together, first eating at a little bistro a few miles away in Dublin, then out here on the porch, drinking wine. I'd given up cigarettes after the fire, but Dottie had brought a joint along with her, and we'd smoked it. Before the topic of the fire came up I had started to feel an unaccustomed warmth, a level of comfort I hadn't experienced in a long time, and I was wondering if it would be okay to kiss her. Now I had to think of a lie to tell her.

"I was in a house that burned down," I said.

She put her hand over her mouth. "Oh no. What started it?"

"Someone fell asleep with a cigarette in his hand," I lied. "Next thing you know, poof. I was upstairs but got out okay." I held my hands up, displaying scarred palms. "Except for these. Could have been worse."

"Lucky," Dottie said, and put her hand over mine.

"Yeah," I said, and then she leaned in and I did get my kiss. A few weeks later we went to bed together, and by the time six months had gone by, we were engaged. The only times the topic of the fire ever came up were dinner parties or get-togethers with new people who saw the scars on the backs of my hands and wanted to know what happened. Dottie supplied the answer as frequently as I did; it had become her story, too. Over the years I'd added few additional facts…true ones, but vague. Steve's name. Someone died. Things like that.

It was the only lie I'd ever told my wife, the only thing I'd ever *needed* to lie about. I was also aware that the lie was a cancer in my relationship with Dottie. It wasn't *a* thing I had lied to her about; it was *the* thing, and my unwillingness to be honest had nothing to do with Dottie and how she might take the truth.

Only when I came to terms with my own role in Lucy's death would I be capable of dealing honestly with anyone else, even my wife. My knowledge of that basic fact had occurred and recurred so frequently it had taken on the power of the moon, and the tides of my daily dealings with the people I loved rose and fell with my ability to rationalize not only the dishonesty, but all of the untold lies that went along with it.

CHAPTER TWENTY-THREE

Years ago, when Roscoe had recovered enough to be moved, his parents had transferred him to a state-of-the-art burn unit in Stratford, a suburb of New York just over the border into Connecticut. For almost a year after the fire that killed Lucy he'd stayed there, first in a "clean room" to minimize the chance of any contaminants infiltrating his decimated immune system, and then, once his grafts had healed enough, in a private room with a view of a meticulously manicured garden he couldn't stand up to walk through. When I visited him there for the first time three or four years after graduating from Penton, sitting beside his bed in a stiff-backed metal chair that seemed designed to stop anyone from staying too long, I always wondered what it must do to a person to live like that. At best it was a half-life, a living purgatory. The sterile room was everything the Roscoe I knew hadn't been, and though I tried, it was impossible to imagine what must have been going on inside of his mind.

When the doctors had finally deemed him well enough to leave the hospital, his parents took him home to Pennsylvania, and there he'd stayed until his mother and father died in a car accident seven or eight years ago. His father, always the heavy drinker, had worked his way through most of a bottle of Johnnie

Walker Black and then wrapped his BMW around a telephone pole. He'd been killed outright; Roscoe's mother, on the other hand, had lasted almost a month in the local ICU, her skull full of holes the doctors drilled to relieve the pressure on her brain.

Within a month of their deaths Roscoe had sold the house in Pennsylvania and purchased a townhouse in Stratford, Connecticut. When I asked him why over the phone, he explained that after the fire he'd never felt comfortable in his home town, and that the only place where he'd been treated like a normal human being since the fire was at the burn unit. Since he still had ties in the hospital and trusted the doctors there, it was the only place it had occurred to him to go.

As I exited I-95 and made my way toward his chintzy subdivision, I thought again about what his life must have been like all these years. If mine had been hard and sometimes unhappy, his had been as close to a living hell as I could imagine.

***

I pulled up in front of Roscoe's house and sat still for a moment, listening to the engine tick as it settled. Because Roscoe's parents had been wealthy and because he had been an only child, their passing had left him able to pick and choose where he would live. He had selected Coventry Gardens, a quiet gated community an hour outside New York City.

Climbing out of the car, the crisp air chilled the sweat on my forehead and I realized for the first time that I was soaked with perspiration. *Calm down*, I told myself. *You've been here before. It's only Roscoe.*

But even as I tried to convince myself of the truth of those sentiments, I knew I didn't believe they were entirely true. This time it wasn't just Roscoe. It was Roscoe and Steve and Lucy and me again. Just like before. As much as I wanted to tell myself that things hadn't changed for me in any essential way, here I was a hundred and twenty miles from home, visiting a friend I only

150

came to see around Christmas and sometimes on his birthday. I wiped my forehead with a hand and then made my way up the wooden ramp to his door.

It was answered on the first knock by Joanna, the live-in nurse who had been with Roscoe for the last five years or so. She was a pleasant-looking fortyish woman who seemed to genuinely care for him, as difficult as he could be to tolerate.

"Paul!" she said, stepping forward to give me a hug. "What are you doing here? Not that it isn't wonderful to see you, but I didn't know you were coming."

As soon as she said the words I realized that I hadn't called ahead. I'd been too preoccupied by other thoughts, and I had been pretty sure that Roscoe would be at home, anyway. The only time he left the house was for doctor appointments.

"I hope it's not a problem," I said. "I was just passing through town and thought I'd take the chance you two would be here."

She slapped me playfully on the arm and clucked. "You're bad."

I smiled sheepishly and asked if Roscoe was awake.

"Sure is," she said, pointing a thumb over her shoulder. "You'll find his majesty in the den watching television. As usual."

"Okay."

As I started in the direction of the den, Joanna said, "It's good of you to come, Paul. Almost no one does. Every time you come by, he's better for weeks."

"He hasn't been doing well lately?"

"Not since your friend was here the other day."

"Friend?" I said, my breath catching in my throat. "Do you remember what his name was?"

"Another friend from college, I think. Stan, or—"

"Steve?"

She nodded. "That's right, Steve. I talked to him for a minute or two when he showed up and he mentioned you, said all of you were friends back in the day. Anyway, tell his eminence it's bath time when you leave. That ought to brighten him right up."

I nodded and headed for the den.

CHAPTER TWENTY-FOUR

He sat in his wheelchair perhaps three feet in front of the TV, the volume off. His head was tilted away from me and I couldn't tell if he was asleep or awake. Blue and white light from the TV flashed on his face.

"Roscoe," I said softly, and he jerked. His hand found the clear plastic mask dangling from the arm of the chair. He raised it to his mouth and sucked, then removed it.

"Who is that?" he said, his voice gravelly from the smoke and heat that had shredded his vocal cords.

"It's me," I said. "Paul."

He shuddered in a breath with significant effort. "Come closer, wouldya?" he said. "Fucking eyes don't work right. They get used to the TV and then it takes half a goddamned hour to see anything else."

Roscoe always spoke of his body this way since the fire, like it was his nemesis. If it wasn't his eyes, it was his legs, which the fire had left largely untouched but which had, in the months and then years he'd spent in hospital beds, atrophied to pitiful and useless straws, the tendons and ligaments drawing in on themselves like old rubber bands. If he had wanted he could have worked on strengthening them again. There was nothing wrong with the muscles that couldn't be undone with sufficient time in the gym with a physical therapist, but he had no interest in walking or running anymore. I suspected that Roscoe wanted to look the way he felt, crippled and useless.

The flickering screen of the television told me that, despite the countless cosmetic surgeries he'd undergone, not much had changed. The skin of his face on the left side looked like a patchwork quilt of grafts. Though the right side had been largely spared, the heat of the fire had burned the vision completely out of his right eye; it moved with the other, but it did so covered by a milky white film. As I approached, Roscoe used the control stick on his chair to rotate it around toward the couch, and I sat down there.

"Hey, old friend," I said.

He sucked again on oxygen from the mask and then said, "Why the visit, Paco? I didn't know you were coming." He licked his lips, which were always dry.

"Steve came to see me last night," I told him. "I thought maybe he was looking for someone to talk him out of killing himself. I can't stop thinking about it."

Roscoe nodded slowly, taking it in. "He was here, too. Couple days ago."

"Joanna told me. She said you've been a little preoccupied since then."

Roscoe sat for a moment, then sucked from the mask. "Preoccupied," he said. "That's a word for it, I guess."

"What'd he say?"

"He wanted to talk about going to Philly to see you."

"That's it?"

"There were other things, too. He's not doing well, Paco."

I waited for him to continue, but he didn't. If he wanted to let me in on whatever had passed between him and Steve, he would. Pushing him wouldn't help. I searched Roscoe's face for some hint of what he was thinking or feeling, and saw only a titanic sadness there, hidden beneath the melted mask of his features.

We sat in silence for a while, and I heard Joanna in another part of the house, the kitchen from the sound of it. All of the blinds on the windows were drawn and the light was dim and yellowish. I could imagine the clean air outside, the brisk wind, the *aliveness* of it, and suddenly I wanted desperately to be out there, out of this stuffy room. I shifted in my seat on the couch.

"What did Steve tell you?" Roscoe said.

"That's just it," I said. "It seemed like he wanted to say something, but he just never got to it. I've been trying to get my head around it, but all I keep coming back to is that he was trying to say goodbye, or that he was looking for help."

"That's not it," Roscoe said, regarding me out of the corner of his good eye.

"What do you mean?"

He shook his head. "You have to hear it from him."

I opened my mouth to say something, but then closed it. Roscoe had always been my truest friend. When I first saw him months after the fire, he hadn't been angry that I'd stayed away as long as I did. Instead, the only emotion I picked up from him was relief. I owed him for that, for forgiving me when I couldn't forgive myself.

"Roscoe," I said, "come on. What am I supposed to do here?"

"Go see him."

"Go all the way to Ohio? But you can just tell me yourself. Why the hell—?"

"I'm not going to tell you anything," Roscoe said. "That's the last thing in the world you'd *want* me to do if you knew what this was about. I won't do it."

I nodded slowly, trying to think of what I could say that would make him change his mind. I started to say something else, then realized it would be useless. Roscoe had made up his mind.

"I found his address online," I said.

"That's what he told me," Roscoe said. "In his folks' old place. Danbury, I think, near Cincinnati." He paused, and pulled from his mask. "Are you going to go?"

"I guess I have to."

"I think so, too," he said, then changed tack and asked me about Dottie and Naomi, about how things were going at the magazine. Because of his condition, he had never been to visit us in Philadelphia. That was in many ways easier for me.

We talked about nothing for a few minutes, but both of us realized that we were skirting the truth. It was difficult to talk to Roscoe about his own life since nothing ever changed. For a long while, back in the years immediately following the fire, I hoped that would change, that he would reinsert himself into the flow of the world somehow, maybe get into physical therapy and counseling sessions. I think if he had done those things in the years just after the fire he could have earned himself a modicum of normalcy. Instead, he'd pulled more and more inside of himself. As much as I hated seeing him this way, I couldn't blame him.

I stood up to go. Roscoe drew in a breath that wheezed through his ruined throat with a dry whistle. "Christmas is soon. Come back, okay?"

"Of course," I said. "I'll be here."

When I left, I got back on the interstate and headed south, knowing that I could be in Ohio in six or seven hours.

PART III

FINALS. HOME WITH LUCY. ROSCOE'S FARM.
THE SHOOT.

CHAPTER TWENTY-FIVE

Sometimes, in a flash of memory that is completely unbidden, I will feel Lucy on top of me, will feel the rush of myself into her body, her lips on mine, and then I will see her as she looked after the fire, her body limp, eyes closed, face smudged and streaked with ash and dirt. The juxtaposition of those images is something that my mind has done to me…that it *still* does. I have always felt it is the least I deserve.

***

When we arrived back at Penton from our Thanksgiving in Swarthmore, both Lucy and I were jittery from the long car ride. A lot had happened over the last few days, but I hadn't really processed it until we'd been afforded the peace of the car during the trip home. Being with Lucy felt right, not because she was the same as me, but because she was nothing like me. I found that I had begun to think in terms of us, and I had to wonder what she was thinking.

We dressed warmly and set off through the cold and dry November evening toward town to stop in at Buns for a quick dinner. The hostess seated us near a window that overlooked the sidewalk. There were white lights in the trees outside and couples walking arm-in-arm. As soon as we sat down, I wished we were back outside.

"What?" Lucy said, following my gaze.

"Hmm?" I said.

"Anxious?"

"Why would I be anxious?"

She shrugged. "I don't know. Why would you?"

"Okay," I said. "Maybe a little jumpy. Nervous."

"Give me that," she said, and held her hand out for my cigarette, keeping the other one on top of mine. I knew that she did so very purposefully, and that when it was time to talk about something else, she would signal me by removing her hand, or simply by changing the pressure of it on my own. For the time being, she felt relaxed and warm.

She exhaled a jet of smoke toward the ceiling and said, "Maybe this is as good a time as any. You have every right to be a little off balance when it comes to me. What do you want to know?"

"You and Steve," I said.

"Okay." Her hand tensed momentarily on top of mine, and I thought for a moment that she would take it away. But as I watched her face, I saw her very consciously try to relax, and her touch softened.

"He's a friend," I said, "and I know it'll bother him, you and me being together."

"I'm sure it will," she said. "But we shouldn't hide it. That would be worse. It would be…insulting."

"That's what I was thinking, too." I paused, trying to think about how to say what I wanted to get out there. "I guess what I want to know is if there's anything I need to know about all of that. It's not my business what happened between you and him, but I don't want to step on any mines, I guess, is the best way of putting it."

"Neither do I," she said. "Steve's a good guy. We've known

each other since high school." She paused, obviously thinking about what to say and how to say it. "We dated for a while when I got to college and then we stopped, but we always stayed close. He took care of me when I couldn't really take care of myself. I was a burden to him. He didn't see it that way, of course, but it's the truth. The more he tried to help me, the more I saw that I was hurting him. It was bad, and it had to end. At the same time…I don't know if I'd still be here without him."

I nodded. "You know he still has a thing for you."

"Paul…." She seemed to reconsider what she'd been about to say. "Yes, I'm aware of that. He's had girlfriends since we were together, but I still see that look in his eye when I'm around him sometimes. It's not because he wants to be with me again. We both know how badly that would turn out. It's because he doesn't want *anyone else* to be with me. Do you know what I mean?"

I flashed back to the night I'd met Lucy, during the party at the abandoned mansion. When Lucy and I had been chosen to go into the closet together, I hadn't understood the look on Steve's face, but there had been something strange about it. What I'd misinterpreted as fear or concern had more likely been suppressed anger and frustration. There had also been the time I'd seen Steve drive off the guy dressed as Dracula at the Halloween party when he tried to give Lucy a beer. I thought about all the hours Steve and I had spent together over the past semester, and felt my spirits drop. Steve *was* a good guy, and I felt terrible about how he'd react when he learned about me and Lucy.

"Hey," Lucy said, snapping me from my thoughts. "It's okay, you know? I mean, what are we supposed to do, *not* be together because it might make someone feel weird for a little while? That's ridiculous. I give Steve more credit than that. He's a big boy. He'll handle it."

I wasn't sure about that, but I wanted to be. "It's just going to be strange."

She shrugged and then smiled at me. "So it'll be strange. Small price."

***

Later that night we walked home through lightly falling snow. We'd seen *Witness* at the Strand, and about halfway though, the fatigue that our nervous tension had held at bay for the last few hours settled in, and both of us fell asleep.

Because there was still one day of break left, Smith was sparsely populated, and we passed no one on the way up to my room. As we trudged up the stairs to the third floor, I could think of nothing but how good it was going to feel to climb into my crowded, single bed with Lucy and curl up under the quilt. Maybe when we woke up in the morning there would be other benefits to spending the night together, but for now, sleep was the only thing on my mind.

Someone was playing Paul Simon in a room down the hall, and someone, maybe the same someone, was smoking pot. Unable to think of anything but bed, I unlocked my door and made my way to the bed, pulling Lucy along with me.

***

Roscoe woke us up the next morning when he came barging through the door, slamming it open with his typical brand of disregard for anything he didn't own.

"Oh, shit," he said when he saw us in bed, still huddled under the covers, my arm wrapped around Lucy from behind. I waited for him to modify the statement, but he just gaped in our general direction, seemingly incapable of further speech.

"Why 'Oh, shit'?" I finally asked.

"Because this is going to make things complicated," he answered, sitting down in the chair behind my desk.

"For you?"

"No, you idiot." He shook his head. "For Steve. You guys must—"

161

"We've already talked about that," Lucy said, her voice still groggy with sleep. "We're going to go see him up at the house sometime soon."

"You sure that's a good idea?" Roscoe asked.

"As opposed to what?" I said. "Sneaking around behind his back like nothing's going on? How would that be any better?"

Roscoe held up his hands. "Hey, don't get pissed at me. I think it's great you two are shacking up. Really, it's about time you got some stink on your hang-low, Paco. I just wanted to make sure you'd given this whole situation some thought, which you obviously have. Fantastic. Really. Now that we've gotten all that shit straight, who wants to get some breakfast with me? I could eat a cow."

The three of us walked into Penton and ate an artery-hardening breakfast at the Hamburger Inn, drowning the eggs, bacon, sausage, and toast with cup after cup of steaming coffee. Whatever reservations Roscoe might have held about my new relationship with Lucy, he kept to himself. Maybe he'd just gotten them all out of his system back in the room. I hoped so. When we finished eating, Lucy told me that she had to get some things done before classes started on Monday. She kissed me goodbye and then headed back toward campus.

I watched her until she turned the corner onto Spring Street and moved out of sight behind the student union.

"You got it *bad*," Roscoe said, his voice pulling me from my thoughts.

Turning to him, I saw that he was smiling, his eyebrows lifted in delight. "Maybe," I said, "but there are worse things. You know?"

He nodded. "It's probably not worth asking you for details."

"Probably not," I said.

***

By the time I got back to Smith I was tired again, and more

162

than anything I just wanted to get back into bed and sleep. But there was work to be done; two hundred pages of reading for my psych class had gone completely ignored during the trip to Philly. Fighting the pull of the rumpled bed, I decided that a shower might help me wake up.

When I walked back into our room ten minutes later, toweling my hair off, some of the fuzziness had gone from my mind. Roscoe was sitting on my bed drinking from a bottle of whiskey.

"Want to go up to the house?" he said.

I took a look at the psych book lying open on my desk, listened for a moment as my conscience see-sawed, then said, "Why not?"

CHAPTER TWENTY-SIX

Even from across the hill the music was loud, as were the voices raised to be heard above it. Someone had taken it upon themselves to rig string upon string of colored Christmas lights around the front pillars and porch railings. From a distance the house looked festive, and as we crunched over the thin crust of snow and ice that had formed atop the grass, I couldn't help but think how different things might actually be once we found Steve. Still, I was eager to get everything out in the open, even if doing so meant more conflict.

Roscoe pushed through a throng of kids holding red plastic cups of beer, and I trailed behind him, like a halfback following his blocker. Moving up through the crowded stairwell we passed several brothers, and though I knew it was probably just my own nerves, I could have sworn all of them saw me and then looked away. Though the air in the house was hot and thick with the moisture pouring off sweating bodies, I felt suddenly cold and a little claustrophobic. Roscoe pushed open the door to the second floor and we exited the stairwell and entered the jam-packed second floor.

The door to Steve's room stood wide open, and Steve was sitting on his couch, a bottle of PBR in his hand, a pretty blonde-haired girl sitting on the couch beside him. His hand rested on her thigh. Half a dozen more students I didn't recognize sat on the floor, at his desk, on the trunk in the corner. There was apparently a drinking game of some kind going on, and it took a moment for Steve to notice that we were standing in his doorway. Finally he glanced up. And smiled.

"Hey, guys, come on in." He got to his feet and extended his hand. After a confused moment, I took it. His grip was warm and friendly, and I found myself more confused than ever. Part of me had fully expected Steve to slam the door in my face.

Steve looked from me to Roscoe, then back to me. Still holding my hand in his own, he pulled me toward him, leaned in, and whispered in my ear.

"Sorry about what I said before break, man," he said, and I could hear what sounded like real sincerity in his voice. "I can be a little protective of Lucy, and you caught me off guard, you know?"

I backed slowly away. "That's okay."

"I mean it, man," Steve continued. "I had no right. I feel like an asshole. Been thinking about it a lot. You guys want a beer?"

"Sure," I said. "I need to talk to you, though. About me and Lucy."

He nodded slowly, and I could see him thinking. He leaned in so his face was a foot from mine. "Are you together?"

"Yes." I tried to read his face, but his expression was flat.

"Okay," he said, nodding, then turned away and stepped back toward the couch and the blonde girl sitting there. Thinking he was done with me, I was about to leave when I heard him say, "Hey, Paco, you want that beer?"

He was holding a bottle out toward me, and I took it. "Thanks."

Roscoe and I stayed with Steve in his room for an hour or so, chatting about school and Steve's movie, and very pointedly avoiding any conversation about what any of us had done during Thanksgiving break. I watched his face in what I hoped was an inconspicuous way, trying to figure out what he was thinking, but he was impossible to read. That fact unto itself was disturbing; from what I'd seen of Steve the past few months, he wasn't one to hide his hand. At a little after nine, Steve's phone rang and he was summoned to the president's room for some kind of official business.

Thoroughly confused, I followed Roscoe back out of the house, knowing only one thing for sure: the feeling of ease I'd had with Steve in the past was gone. Even if we could figure out a way to make our friendship work now, and it seemed like Steve was keeping that door open, our relationship was going to be stained with a new seriousness I would have to learn to live with.

***

In the following weeks things became more complicated. The rhythms I'd established at school were thrown out of whack as Lucy and I took every free moment to be together. I went to bed later and woke up later, missed classes when I decided I'd rather spend that time with Lucy, neglected completing the occasional assignment. It wasn't the kind of thing that could go on long term, but for the time being, that new level of complexity seemed a fair trade. When we went up to Sigma Theta together I sometimes felt like Steve's closest friends looked at me differently, not so much directly as out of the corner of the eye. Jerome and Dan were exceptions. They treated me the same as they always had, which was to say they treated me like someone to drink with. I was fine with that.

Steve was the same old Steve. Whatever resentment I'd expected from him as a result of my relationship with Lucy, it failed to materialize. Instead, we quickly resumed our old rapport. Mostly we worked on the script, tweaking and planning. We talked props and rudimentary storyboards, took notes on a few scenes where particular camera angles seemed to be warranted. We ate fried food from the kitchen and drank Pabst Blue Ribbon beer and laughed and talked, and it felt fine.

The one script obstacle we had the most difficulty working out was offered a quick and easy solution one night in early December as Roscoe, Steve, and I sat drinking beer in his room.

"What we need," Steve was saying, "isn't more actors... we've got that covered, I think. What we *need* is a solid location for the barn shoot."

If the movie was going to work out the way we wanted, it would need to take place inside a convincingly barn-like structure, and though there *were* plenty of barns around Penton, all of them were in use. Even if we went in at night to work, we would have to pay for use of the property.

I shrugged. "There's that old place out on route thirty-six that could work. It's a little beat-up, but if we got the shots from the right angles...."

"I guess," Steve said, and sighed. "But fuck, a good barn could make this look *authentic*, you know?"

Roscoe, who to this point had mostly sat in silence, suddenly spoke up. "I know a barn you could use."

Both of us turned to look at him, and he smiled.

"It's a little out of the way, but it's empty, and it would be free to shoot in."

"Where?" Steve asked.

Roscoe took a sip of his beer, leaned back in his seat on the couch, and said, "Calderville, Pennsylvania."

As it turned out, Roscoe's family was wealthy, but hadn't always been so. In fact, it was only in the last two generations of the Ballentemps family that they had joined the ranks of the *nouveau riche*, a result of a trucking business Roscoe's grandfather had used to build a small fortune, which had been buttressed later by some savvy investments Roscoe's own father made long before Roscoe's birth.

As the Ballentemps clan came to the gradual conclusion that the source of their monetary income wasn't going to dry up overnight, they moved out of the poor rural community in western Pennsylvania where they'd lived for generations and into the city. But they never sold the old homestead. Instead they'd refurbished it, converting it into a vacation retreat of which the family never made much use. The old place came complete with a barn.

Steve sat back in his seat, a pensive look on his face. "We could do it," he said, "but we'd have to get everyone over there."

"Christmas Break," I said. "We could probably shoot what we need in three or four days. We can get it done before Christmas, I think." Though I was trying hard to control my excitement, from the way Roscoe had described the property, and the barn in particular, it sounded perfect. Steve and I had planned the movie as well as we could, had spent hours trimming the script and working out the minutia of each scene, and now that we'd been offered this chance to work on such an isolated location, a place where we could go about our business undisturbed, the last piece seemed to have fallen into place.

Steve said, "Let me get in touch with everyone and see how they feel." He looked at Roscoe, concerned. "This isn't going to cause problems with you and your dad, is it?"

"Fuck him," Roscoe said. "He doesn't even have to know. I have a key, and they sure as hell won't head out there in the middle of winter."

"Okay," Steve said. "Let's see what we can do."

***

Every free moment we had, Lucy and I spent together. Before long we had each others' class schedules memorized, and we'd meet at the union for coffee before walking to the academic side of campus together, where I could drop her at the her morning

Psych or English class before heading off to the lecture that would separate us for an hour or two. Dinners we alternated between the dining halls in Smith and the student union, but just as often we used cash to buy groceries at the small store in the basement of Thompson Hall and spent the evening eating canned spaghetti or soup on the couch in my room and studying side-by-side.

I was very conscious of the way in which the rest of the world was receding from my vision. When I'd arrived at college just a few months earlier, there had seemed to be a multitude of choices to make. The freedom that college presented seemed almost overwhelming. Now I felt the exact opposite, but in the most extraordinary way. I felt wanted and comfortable; I felt *found*. There were no rules in my life but those I decided to follow, and in this respect, my relationship with Lucy was the truest freedom I'd ever known.

CHAPTER TWENTY-SEVEN

The week before school let out for Christmas Break, Lucy and I were sitting in her room, each of us engrossed in our books. Or so I thought. I looked up to find her staring at me. She was twirling a strand of hair around a finger.

"What?" I said.

"My parents called last night," she said, shifting in her seat, where she'd been nestled for the past hour in a tightly curled position that no male could ever hope to emulate.

I put down my book. Lucy never talked about her parents.

"They want me to come home for Christmas. I said I was involved in Steve's project and that I'd call them back when I knew my schedule."

For a moment I said nothing, just sat quietly, waiting to see where she was going with this. When she didn't speak again immediately, I said, "It shouldn't be a problem. Filming won't take more than three or four days. That leaves almost two weeks."

Lucy nodded. "You haven't said what you're planning on doing."

I shrugged. "To be honest, I was hoping you'd come home with me again. My parents love you." Had she not broached the topic, there would have been no way around my doing so in the next couple of days, if just so I could tell my mom and dad whether or not to purchase a plane ticket for me.

Lucy shifted again, looking more uncomfortable than ever. "They'd let me come again? Seriously?"

"Are you kidding? My mom wants to adopt you." It may have been an exaggeration, but only a slight one. I'd talked to my parents a couple of times since Thanksgiving, and each time my mother had asked if Lucy was with me and if she could say hello.

There were suddenly tears in her eyes. "Let's do that then. We can go to Roscoe's farm and then to your house. I don't want to be in that house with those people."

"Your parents?"

Nodding, she wiped at her eyes with the back of her hand. "It would make things so much easier, not to have to go there."

I pushed myself out of the chair in which I'd been sitting and went to her, knelt in front of the couch, and put my hands on either side of her face. She felt hot and shaky. "We can do whatever you want, Luce." I lifted one of her hands from her lap and kissed the back of it, tasting the salty tears from her cheeks.

Lucy put her book aside and wrapped her arms around my neck and kissed me. What could make someone feel this way about her parents? It was a useless question to ask myself, but even Roscoe, who when he went home had to face a living hell, showed some affection toward his mother and father.

I picked her up and carried her to her bed, and by the time we had gotten each other undressed, her shaking had nearly stopped.

***

The period during which we took our final exams came and went with a blurry, greasy kind of speed. For a week long period eating became a luxury, drinking alcohol an impossibility, and smoking cigarettes, one pack after the next, practically a way of life.

On the first day of finals Roscoe and I walked down to Barrows Hall, where we were both scheduled to take our exams in Freshman Composition. All night long we'd quizzed each other back and forth about Joyce and Melville. We'd spent two hours covering the various figurative attributes of *Huckleberry Finn*, a good portion of which we'd spent laughing at the horrible critical piece our professor had assigned us to read after we finished the book; "Huckleberry the Feminist," the essay had been called.

Now, as we neared Barrows, I could practically feel the waves of anxiety coming off of Roscoe. Part of it was exams, but I knew he was also dreading seeing his parents. He'd seemed distracted all morning, ever since fielding a call from home that had roused us both from bed.

I felt terrible suddenly, terrible as a person, terrible as a friend. Since Lucy and I had started spending more time with each other, I'd seen less of Roscoe. There was nothing intentional about it; I'd seen little of anyone else, either. My world had simply constricted, closed in on me until it seemed there was only space for two. I shut my eyes and tried to breathe out some of the crummy feeling in my heart. When I opened them again, Roscoe was looking at me.

"You okay, man?" he said.

"Sure," I said, then we went inside to take our test.

***

After my last exam on Friday of that week, I walked back to Smith and found the room empty. A piece of white paper sat on my unmade bed, and on top of the paper, a silver key. I picked up the note. It said:

Paco, my mom called and said that my grandmother took a bad fall and can't get around by herself anymore at all, so I have to go home early. Sorry, I know we were going to put back a few after tests tonight. Here's the key to the house. Eat whatever you want. The pantry's always full. Good luck with everything, man. If I can get away to come see you

172

guys, I'll do it.

Later, Roscoe.

PS. The phone up there isn't connected, so if you need to make a call, you have to drive into town.

Below the note, Roscoe had left a series of directions.

"Thanks, man," I said to the empty room.

CHAPTER TWENTY-EIGHT

Since Roscoe was gone and I didn't have to worry about ditching him our last night at school, Lucy and I spent the night in her room. We ordered pizza from Tim's and sat on the floor eating a greasy pepperoni pie and drinking beer. With my pocket knife, I sliced the top off one of the cans and we used it as an ashtray.

Since we'd come back to school from our visit with my parents, Lucy and I had been spending more and more time in her dorm room. For one thing, it was bigger, and her bed was more comfortable than mine. She kept it layered with cushy quilts, and tucked a down comforter beneath the fitted sheet. My bed in Smith sagged so pathetically in the middle that it sometimes felt as though we were sleeping in a hammock; Lucy's bed was soft but firm, and my lower back, which had started to ache on a daily basis since I'd arrived at Penton, had never felt better. For another thing, Lucy had a single, so there was no worrying that Roscoe might suddenly show up at an inopportune moment.

It had taken so long for Lucy to invite me to her room that I had begun to conjecture wildly about what it would be like. The inside of her car was the only thing I had to go on, so part of me thought it would be filthy. Again, I'd been surprised.

Her room was feminine and comfortable. Where Roscoe and I had a room full of hard metal and plastic chairs and desks and bunks, Lucy had disposed of the shoddy furniture Penton supplied and filled her living space with antiquey-looking pieces. A delicate wooden side table next to a comfortable second-hand couch; chairs that looked like they might have come straight out of a country kitchen; a low-to-the-ground coffee table that filled the middle of her room. Her walls were covered with framed posters, mostly movie ads and stills. The wall over my desk back in Smith was layered with a collage of taped up photos of friends and family, but Lucy had none of those. In one of my more intrepid moments I'd asked her why, and she'd told me there was no one worth remembering from home. That's all the answer she was willing to give, and I thought it was probably all I needed. I knew Lucy had waited so long to bring me to her room because she was so intensely private; these were exactly the types of things she didn't want to explain. I'd learned that she would talk when she was ready, and that it was useless and actually harmful to push.

"Are you okay with leaving at around noon tomorrow?" Lucy said as she blotted the top of a slice with a paper towel.

I finished chewing and said, "Sure. From Roscoe's directions, it looks like two hours or so."

"Okay." For a moment she was quiet, then, "I called my parents and told them I wasn't coming."

"What did they say?"

"Not much. I called when I knew my dad would be at work, and my mom never says anything."

She looked like she was about to say something else, but didn't. I realized then that Lucy Carpenter, who had somehow become my girlfriend, was in many respects like a sprawling house, but one where all the doors were locked. The question you had to ask yourself was whether searching for the keys to

175

open those doors was worth the price. This time I thought maybe she was trying to open one of the doors for me, so I decided to push a little.

"What?" I asked.

She shook her head. "Nothing. I was just thinking that I don't remember my mother saying anything other than 'yes,' 'no,' and 'okay' in forever. Then again, I haven't really been home in years."

"You didn't go home last summer?"

"Steve was going out west to take a tour around Yellowstone and the Grand Canyon, so I went with him. He has family in Nevada, so we stayed with them for a couple of weeks while we were out there. The trip took almost the entire summer, and I was thankful for it. If I had to spend the summer at home, I'm not sure I would have made it."

Fighting a mixture of jealousy and resentment that had suddenly sprung to life inside me, I said, "What do you mean?"

Lucy dropped her pizza back in the box and leaned back on her straightened arms. "Do you trust me, Paul?"

"Of course. Why?"

"I was thinking about how I've always kept things from you, things I haven't been willing to talk about. That's unfair. You just get into these habits, you know?"

"It's your life. Those things have nothing to do with me. If you want me to know, you'll tell me."

"I will," she said, resting her hand on my thigh. "You deserve to know. More than anyone else in my life, I feel like I can tell you about those things, but it scares me."

"Why?" I asked, taking her hand with my own.

"Because...I don't know." She turned her face away from me, looking out the window. The forecast had been for a fairly substantial storm, and already a light snow had started to fall.

"Because what?"

176

When she spoke them, her words were all but inaudible. "Because, what if you hate me?"

"That's impossible."

There was a knock at the door, but Lucy seemed not to hear it. "It's not. I've done things—"

Another knock, this time louder, more insistent. Whoever it was obviously wasn't just going to go away.

"Do you want me to get that?" I asked.

"Okay," Lucy said. She stood up, too, and walked to the window, still stuck wherever she had gone in her own mind.

I opened the door and found myself looking at a man in his late forties or early fifties, his gray-black hair wind-tossed and flaked with unmelted snow. More snow had dampened his black coat. He wore a blue and white striped dress shirt, a tie pulled loose and crooked. The smell of hard liquor wafted into my face, and I felt the smile I'd been wearing falter.

"Hi," I said, confused. "Can I help you?"

The man looked over my shoulder, his brow furrowed. "Lucy," he said.

Behind me I heard her feet on the floor, then her voice. It sounded hard in a way I'd never heard it, like a closed door. "Why are you here?" she said. "I called and told Mom—"

"I know what you told her," Lucy's father said over my shoulder. "But you're still coming home. Get your things together. Get your things together *now*."

I turned to look at Lucy, my hand still on the doorknob. She was standing a few feet behind me, her face pale but composed.

"No," she said. She took a step back as she said it, whether to signal her choice to stay or out of simple anxiety.

As though I was watching some kind of verbal tennis match, I turned back to her father and saw him take a deep breath, then raise both hands over his head and slap them against the doorframe. His face was to the ground, but I could hear the sound

177

of his breathing, loud and deep and raspy, like an animal, a bear or a bull, something preparing to charge. Another powerful wave of whiskey-stench assaulted my nostrils, and I stepped back without thinking about it.

Very slowly, Lucy's father raised his head. There was an unbalanced, crazed look in his eyes. My mind made a strange connection, drawing from something in my childhood, and I thought, *it's the minotaur.* I saw wetness at the corners of his mouth, and his lips kept coming together then popping back open again. I took another step away, feeling a clench of fear in my belly.

"Get in the car, Lucy," her father said. "I'm not leaving here without you in the car. Get in the car. Get in the CAR!" He slammed a hand into the doorframe and I felt the vibration in the floor. A strand of spittle now hung from his lower lip and was stretching toward the front of his coat.

"Hey, look...," I said, trying to figure out what role to play here.

He dropped his hands from the door and stepped into the room, panting now, his eyes too wide and bloodshot. "You do *not* speak to me. You do not say *words* into my face, you dumb shit. There are no *words* you can say to me!" His hand lashed out and pounded the door into the wall.

From behind me Lucy spoke. I could hear her trying to make her voice sound bored and disinterested, but to me she sounded like a bad actress speaking bad lines. "Just leave, Father. I'm not going anywhere with you."

Everything after that happened so quickly that I'm still not certain about the exact sequence of events. I remember seeing Lucy's father's bloodshot eyes widen, bulge like he was too full of something red, and then I was on the ground and he was past me and my head slammed into something. Purple flowers blossomed in my eyes and I brought a hand in front of my face

178

and saw red on my fingers. *What happened?* I thought. *Did he hit me?* And then I don't remember anything for a little while other than dulls swirls of color and bright static, and then a surge of liquid blackness that leaked in from the edges of my vision and swallowed me up.

When I got up I felt sick to my stomach and the room was empty, the door wide open. I lurched forward and got there before the world went sideways, and I was suddenly on the ground again, out in the hallway now, the heels of both hands stinging from carpet burn. I gained my feet and staggered to the elevator, and pressed the button for the lobby when the car came. The world rotated like I had a terrible case of the spins, and I braced myself with a hand against the wall. The back of my shirt collar was sticky and cold, and I could feel more wetness on my back, between my shoulder blades. The back of my head burned like someone had set my hair on fire. When the elevator door opened in the lobby, I tried my best to run to the door that opened into the parking lot, going purely on instinct, unsure how long I had been unconscious, or if I'd ever really blacked out at all. Maybe Lucy's father had taken her and gone an hour ago. I didn't know.

The cold wind that hit me when I stepped outside was cruel, but helped, too, if only a little. I felt my head clear a bit, and I took a deep breath and surveyed the lot in front of me, grasping the frigid rail in a hand already shaking from exposure.

The snow that had started to fall before was coming down more heavily now, and it was hard to see too far. Flakes of snow swarmed around the arc sodium lamps in the parking lot like angry moths, and cut off the glow after it had traveled only a few feet. There weren't many cars in the lot, however, and I ran toward the first one I saw.

As I neared it, I saw Lucy and her father materialize from the blowing frenzy and my heart jolted. I was too far away to hear

179

what they were saying, but I heard Lucy scream and she was struggling to get away from him. He had a grip on her upper arm but she spun away from him, shucked out of the coat she was wearing, and then she was free and running. She was still wearing her slippers and her feet skidded in the new snow as she sprinted away from him, but she stayed on her feet and raced toward the street.

"Lucy!" I yelled, "Stop!" But either she didn't hear me or didn't dare stop to turn and look, because she took off across the street in the direction of Grady Street. I sprinted after her, the pain in my head forgotten, and was halfway across the street when her father's car nearly ran me down.

The car's headlights were off and he took the turn onto Grady way too fast, bumped up over the low curb, and sideswiped a tree. The rear window of the car blew out with a pop and I heard metal crumple. But he gunned the engine again and the tires spun on snow, blowing a plume of white out behind them until they finally hit concrete and gained purchase. The car shot ahead, swerving back and forth as the front tires tried to find a direction.

Halfway down the street I saw Lucy's dark silhouette turn into the entrance to Blue Limestone Park, and then disappear from view behind the row of trees that lined the drive.

Come on, I thought, *don't see her. Go right on by.* I set off at a run and felt the breath stop in my throat as the car's brake lights came on as it reached the park. The car accelerated, though, and a few seconds later blew through a red light as it swerved onto Route 36 and then was gone from sight.

I slid to a stop and caught myself on the sign for Blue Limestone Park, heart beating too fast and not on rhythm, really feeling the cold for the first time. My hands were getting numb, and I was shivering now in my T-shirt and jeans.

"Lucy!" I yelled. "Lucy! Come out! He's gone!"

Nothing.

I looked down and saw a line of tracks, new tracks, heading off into the park, the footprints set far apart. She'd kept on running. Shit. I set off at a jog, the fastest I felt I could move without losing my footing or the trail. I stopped at the park's little playground.

The moon shone down on the park in front of me, lit the swirling snow bright and white. Ahead was a jungle gym, a see-saw, some bars, a red plastic car on a spring. But no Lucy. I yelled her name again, and when there was no answer took a few steps toward the woods that began on the other side of the playground. Then I stopped.

I had progressed from shivering to all-out shaking. I couldn't feel my hands or feet or arms. What had Lucy been wearing? Even less than me, I thought. Jeans and a tank top. Slippers. She had slipped out of the coat to get away from her father.

Panic set in.

What if I couldn't find her before the cold became too much for me? What if she'd been so terrified that she'd gone into the woods to hide, then gotten lost? Jesus, had she really been wearing *only* a tank top and jeans? I couldn't remember.

I had to go back to the room. Had to go back and get a coat for myself and one for Lucy. When I found her she was going to be freezing, and I didn't have anything to warm her with. I had to.

Running, I retraced my steps and made it to the dorm in minutes, then sprinted up the stairs to Lucy's room, ignoring the voice in my head telling me to save some energy, I was going to need it.

Lucy's door was still open and I stepped inside.

"Paul." My head snapped up and I saw Lucy in the bathroom doorway, her face ashen, alarmingly dark smudges beneath her eyes, her lips blue-gray. She was shaking like she might come apart.

"Oh, thank God," I whispered, my voice sounding strange in

181

my own ears. There was black again at the edges of my vision. I sagged to my knees.

"You're bleeding," Lucy said and came to me, kneeling down. "We need to see how bad it is."

I caught her wrist as she reached for my head. "Okay, but in my room. He doesn't know me." I looked at the door, sure that Lucy's father would appear in it any second.

Lucy nodded. "You're right."

The last thing either of us wanted to do was go back out in the cold, but we put on our coats and slipped out the back door of Bashford, our arms around each other for support.

CHAPTER TWENTY-NINE

"Will he go back to your room?" I asked. We sat in the bathroom on the floor, both wrapped in blankets, and Lucy was cleaning the cut on my head with peroxide and wads of gauze. When Lucy's father had knocked me to the floor, I'd rapped my head on the frame of her bed and opened an inch-long gash in my scalp. Nothing too awful in the end, but as scalp wounds will, it hurt and had bled like a bastard. My T-shirt was a goner.

"I don't think so," Lucy said. "If I had to guess, I'd bet he is asleep in a hotel by now."

I hissed in air as Lucy dabbed at my wound. "He was pretty worked up. What makes you think he'll just stop looking for you?"

"It's not about calming down. Drunk as he was, he would have been lucky to get ten miles before he passed out." She sat back and dropped the gauze onto the floor. "Last time he pulled something like this, he broke into my room before I got home from class. I came in and found him drunk as hell, passed out on my bed. This is just what he does."

"When was that?" I asked.

"When do you think?"

I shrugged.

Lucy smiled at me. "Let's just say I'd planned to clean my car out a little before we went to Swarthmore for Thanksgiving, but something came up."

"I had no idea," I said, remembering the day she'd come by Smith to pick me up in her BMW. "I thought you were just sloppy."

Lucy smeared some antiseptic ointment on a finger. "I am," she said, moving closer to me again. "Now, this is probably going to suck."

"Great," I muttered, closing my eyes.

***

It was a little past two in the morning and neither of us could sleep. I'd taken some aspirin, but the headache that had come with the cut on my head wouldn't let go. It didn't help that I could feel Lucy beside me, her body taut as a guitar string. So I asked if she wanted to take a walk.

The snow had all but stopped, and nearly a foot of new powder shifted and swirled in the light of the moon. Against the black of the night, the white was starkly unbroken and pristine. I shrugged deeper into my coat and tightened my grip on Lucy's hand.

As I'd expected there was no one else out, not on this night, not at this hour. We strolled down the middle of Spring Street, dragging our feet through the snow, making long furrows in the powder. I looked back and saw our tracks, side by side, long black tears in white paper. I felt like we were the only two people on the planet, a thought that was as attractive as it was discomfiting.

"I was raped," Lucy said.

I felt myself almost stop in my tracks, but kept moving forward, acted natural. Had I misheard? I couldn't find words to say back.

"It was in high school," she said. "I used to like to go out to parties and drink with friends, the kind of stuff everyone does

184

in high school. One night there was a kegger out at a barn in the country, and I had too much to drink too fast and I got sick and passed out. Someone picked me up and carried me back into a stall and put me on some hay and...."

She stopped, but she didn't have to say anything else. A similar thing had happened to a girl I knew in high school. She drank too much, fell asleep, and when she woke up her skirt was hiked up, her panties nowhere to be found. She had no memory of any of it. The girl had been a friend of Jo's, and every time I saw her after that, I wondered how she could ever trust anyone again.

Lucy looked at me. "I'm telling you this now because it has to do with my father."

"Okay," I said.

"Anyway, I didn't tell anyone for a couple of days, but I couldn't sleep and I didn't want to eat anything. Finally, I felt so sick and looked so bad that my mother kept asking me what was wrong, so I told her what had happened. I told her that a girlfriend of mine had seen a boy carrying me back into the stall then come out a while later, tucking his shirt into his pants. It didn't come out so lucidly at the time, but I told her, and when I did I felt this incredible relief. Just because someone else finally *knew*."

"And then your mom told your dad," I said.

She nodded. "But it turned out the boy was the son of a member of the board of the school where my father works. My father was the head of the upper school, and he had already been there for fifteen years and was next in line to be headmaster. Everyone pretty much knew it was going to be him. Just a matter of time."

I groaned inwardly. "You can't be serious. He didn't say anything to anyone?"

"No," Lucy said

185

Since I had arrived at Penton I'd felt as though I'd learned a great deal about what human beings were capable of. I'd watched Roscoe's antics with booze and girls, sat quietly in a kind of awe as the brothers of Sigma Theta drank and smoked and screwed everything in sight, listened to Lucy's story about Charles Coker, who had manipulated her into doing things that would shatter the self-confidence of any young woman. There was no arguing the fact that I'd been naïve when I got to college, that I hadn't fully understood the depths the human animal could sink to.

But *this.*

A father who learned that his daughter had been raped, but didn't report it to the police, or to *anyone* for that matter. All in the name of a job. I thought of my own parents. There were no lengths they wouldn't go to if someone had hurt me the way Lucy had been hurt. None. What must it do to a person to know their parents weren't there to protect them, to stand up for them when the worst happened?

Everything crystallized for me then. Lucy ceased to be a mystery. I suddenly saw an entire history about which she'd never spoken, could imagine the things she'd done in the years after her father had failed to come to her aid. I didn't need to know the specifics, but Lucy had more to say. My mind was already drawing up variations of its own, showing me what happened to a young girl when she found out her life mattered less than a promotion. There was only one way she could go, and no matter how she went about getting there, that direction was down.

"I'm sure you can picture the way things were at home from then on. I acted out, screamed at my parents, brought boys back to the house. There was one...." Lucy looked down and I knew she wanted to finish and was fighting for what to say. "There was a guy who I forced myself on and I ended up pregnant. Stupid. I think I almost *wanted* it to happen. I got an abortion and made sure both of my parents heard about it, just so they'd know the rumors were out there. When I finally graduated, I came here, hoping things would change. I hated who I was."

I'd never seen someone so full of self-resentment. What she had done to me in the closet of the old mansion, and in Coker's office; they weren't acts of promiscuity, not in any way. The truth behind her motivation was much darker, much sadder. The truth had everything to do with self-preservation and the ugliest kind of betrayal. Although I had been ignorant about all of this, I had been complicit in what we had done, too; knowing that now felt ugly.

"I understand," I said, and I meant any number of things by the statement, too many things to articulate in any way that would mean anything. I felt dirty with knowledge.

"Is it okay if we don't talk about this anymore?" Lucy said. "I wanted you to know, but I'm through."

"Okay," I said.

But in my head I kept talking. I found her father in his hotel room over on the other side of Penton and I told him what he had done to his daughter's heart, how he had nearly destroyed her, what he deserved for his selfishness and heartlessness. It was the best I could do for myself at the time, but I told myself that someday I would find Lucy's father and say the words to his face.

CHAPTER THIRTY

The next morning broke clear and cold, the sky pale blue and cloudless. Plows had been out and the roads were clear.

We drove east, cutting through the rolling Ohio countryside. Lucy slept in the passenger-side seat, her head resting against the window. From time to time we hit bumpy areas of road, but she never so much as stirred. Whatever reserves of energy she kept stored inside her, she'd exhausted them during a morning that hadn't gone well.

I was also tired; in fact, if I hadn't been so concerned with taking care of Lucy, I would have realized that I was actually exhausted. My head still hurt from the knock I'd taken the night before, but it also ached from the rancid thoughts jostling around inside my skull.

Unable to fall back asleep after our walk, Lucy and I decided to go back to her room so she could pack a few things before we left in the morning. We were careful approaching Bashford, first scouting the parking lot from a distance for her father's car, then creeping slowly up the stairwell to the second floor, peeking around corners on the off chance her father had parked elsewhere and was waiting for us to come back. But we were in luck, and he was nowhere to be found. He had left something for Lucy, though.

There was a note written in a furious hand tacked to the bulletin board on the outside of her door. Lucy tore it off and held it out so both of us could see it.

LUCY, I WILL NOT PLAY THIS FUCKING GAME ANYMORE. COME HOME OR YOUR TUITION WILL NOT BE PAID FOR NEXT SEMESTER.

That was it. For a long moment Lucy said nothing, then she crushed the paper into a ball and dropped it on the ground. I closed my eyes. *What an unbelievable bastard.* I looked at Lucy.

"Okay," she whispered, then turned to me. "Let's get me packed."

I felt sick, and a wave of abject sadness took me over. Lucy opened her door and took a duffle bag from her closet, dropped it on her bed, and started rifling through her closet.

"Do me a favor and get some wool socks from my dresser," she said, her voice level and impossible to read. "And my boots. It's going to be cold spending so much time outside. Did you pack enough warm stuff?"

"What?" I asked, confused. "You're coming to Calderville?"

She laughed. "Of course. What, you didn't think that shit was going to work, did you?"

"But what about what he said? Your tuition. Are you sure it's a good idea?"

"He'll pay," she said. "What's he going to tell everyone if I suddenly drop out of school? He can't really go with the truth, that he flat didn't pay my tuition. People at the school wouldn't look too kindly on that, especially not if I started talking, maybe dropped to a couple of my old teachers that Dad just didn't care about my education anymore. He'll pay to keep me quiet, the way he likes me."

I wasn't so sure. The man I'd seen looked anything but rational in the way Lucy had just described. "Are you positive?"

"No. But I'll make his life hell if he tries to go through with it. He knows that. When he sobers up he'll rethink it. Who knows if he'll even remember writing the note when he wakes up?"

And that's where we left it.-

I had given Lucy a copy of the script to read over while we drove, but she'd fallen asleep before she could start; now it rested on the floor of the car between her outstretched legs. It was okay, though. We'd be working piecemeal through the script, and there would be time to explain each scene as we went. Still, part of me hoped she would wake up and take a look before we got to Calderville; I wanted her to see what Steve and I had done.

Gradually the countryside turned into gently sloping hills, and then, as we crossed into Pennsylvania, full-blown mountains. With Lucy still sleeping peacefully next to me, I followed the directions Roscoe had written out, guiding the car along the highway and then smaller, winding country roads at a speed below the posted limit.

Surrounded by quiet, I found myself thinking about things that had obviously been waiting for an opening to present themselves to me, and now they flitted around in my head like a flock of terns. Roscoe's situation was chief among these issues, and I was particularly troubled by it because I could have helped him more. Over the last week before school broke, he had grown increasingly withdrawn and sullen. Sometimes when I found him in the room, sitting and staring into space, I knew that he was thinking about going home for such a long period of time, almost a month. Always I had tried to cheer him up by suggesting that we head out for a while, up to the house or maybe into town, and sometimes he'd even taken me up on those offers. But what I should have done, what a true friend *would* have done, was offer to go home with him or to take him home with me.

But then there was Lucy, who grew more essential to my existence each and every hour. I loved her; it would have been useless to deny that, not that I had any desire to do so. I would have been perfectly happy to lock myself in a room with her and never leave.

Her family situation, which so far I'd only glimpsed for the briefest of moments, seemed equally as terrible as Roscoe's. Still, I couldn't help feeling that, when presented with the choice, I'd chosen the girl over the friend, and that made me feel like crap.

Steve played into my thoughts, too. I liked him, and was grateful for the way he'd handled my relationship with Lucy. I knew it couldn't be easy for him. But no matter how well he *looked* like he was coping with it, no matter the face he wore, it was impossible to believe that he could still feel about me as he had before. I longed for the simplicity of my life as it had been, but I couldn't imagine giving up what I now had.

At just after ten-thirty I saw a sign that read WELCOME TO CALDERVILLE, and turned onto an unpaved lane crowded by pine trees on either side. As the car passed through, low-hanging branches scraped against the door panels, and I hoped what Roscoe's directions were as accurate as he'd promised. Turning around on this road would be next to impossible.

And then, suddenly, the trees were gone.

***

The farmhouse and barn occupied a clearing that was a couple of hundred yards wide in each direction. When the grass had been trimmed and the property tended, the vista was probably serene and pastoral, but now the dead grass was knee-high in the patches where it protruded from the snow, lending the landscape the look of a homeless person with a skin condition. There was more snow here than in Ohio; a foot of fluffy white lay on top of the frozen ground, the brown grass shooting out of it. It sagged the roofline of the farmhouse, long, heavy icicles pulling the gutters away like peeling paint.

The original house, which looked to have been modest,

was still at the center of the amalgamation, like the nucleus of a cell that had sprawled out of control. Several later additions sprouted willy-nilly, and though the house never rose to more than two stories, I had no doubt that the inside would be even more confusing and bizarre than it appeared from the yard.

I guided the car over the unpaved driveway and pulled as close to the porch as I could, then gently touched Lucy's leg.

"We're here."

She stirred and then sat up straighter, wiping at her eyes. "Already?"

"Door-to-door service. Want to go in?"

***

As it turned out, the porch door led not into the front of the house, but into the kitchen. Not that it was possible to identify what part constituted the front, the back, or the side. My own house back in Swarthmore was roomier than this one, but this house was unremitting, endless.

A three-leaf dining table occupied the center of the room, its top thick with gray dust, and a broken down couch and two equally worn easy chairs stood against the wall, all turned toward the center of the room.

"Weird," Lucy said.

"No joke."

Moving in what I hoped was the direction of the original house, we passed through two more of the strange hybrid rooms before finally encountering the kitchen. I set the bag of food down on the kitchen counter.

"Jesus, this place is dirty," I said, wiping a finger through the fluff on the counter, leaving a long, straight line of what almost looked white.

"Didn't Roscoe say they don't come here much?"

I pulled open the fridge door, happy to see that the power was on, at least. "Yeah, though I was under the impression that they kept it up a little."

"Roscoe say that?"

"No," I replied. "But they're rich. You'd think that if they *did* decide to make a trip out here to East Bumfuck, they'd want it clean."

"Want to take a look around?" She raised an eyebrow at me, a brightness in her eyes that hadn't been there just a few hours before. It was as if she became more and more the old Lucy, the Lucy I knew, with each passing moment. My thoughts were still very much on the note her father had left tacked to her door, but Lucy appeared to have put it aside. I took her hand.

"There's only one place I want to go," I said, pulling her toward the kitchen door.

"And that would be?"

"The first bedroom we find."

"Who needs a bedroom?" Her arms went around me and she pulled me to her, buried her face in the space between my throat and jaw, kissed me there, then drew me down to her. I kissed her back, gently at first then harder, feeling pulsing in my body and in hers. Part of me had been worried about how I'd react to Lucy's touch after hearing her story, but my mind took me elsewhere. I felt close to her in a way I never had before.

Lucy wasn't the sum total of the terrible things that had been done to her. She was the product of an entire lifetime. I could imagine her as a young girl, not the kind who hid out in her room playing with dolls and having delicate tea parties with imaginary friends. No, she would have been the little girl running through the woods, the one who wanted to play soccer or football with the boys, even if they didn't want her to play. She was strong and good, and if those parts of her hadn't been properly cared for through the first twenty years of her life, she hadn't let that ruin her. I felt my heart in my throat and tears rose in my eyes. My own life had been one boon after another; it had been easy and simple in a way Lucy's had not. I realized then that the only thing I wanted, the only thing I *needed*, was to be good to her.

"Come here." Holding tightly to my arms, she pulled me down onto the couch. I pulled her shirt off and draped it over the back of the couch, and she added mine to it. Her warm hands were like fire on my chest.

"I love you," I said, eyes closed. "And I'm not going anywhere."

***

We were starving, so we opened cans from the pantry; Chef Boyardee ravioli, French-style green beans, a jar of Vienna sausages, a pack of Saltine crackers, some beans. We sat and ate and drank beer in front of the fireplace after lighting a fire. Lucy wore a blanket over her shoulders. I could see the marks my mouth had made on her shoulder in the light. We didn't speak.

When we finished eating, Lucy stood up and walked from the room. I followed her.

She opened the front door and stepped outside into the cold. A soft snow had begun to fall, and Lucy stuck out her tongue and caught a flake, shrugged the blanket from her shoulders, and held out her arms to me. I took her to me, felt the gooseflesh on her arms and breasts and the heat of her mouth underneath my jaw, on my neck.

I tried to pull her back into the house, but she resisted. She ran her hand down my stomach and found me hard, and stroked me with a hand cool from the air.

"Come on," she said.

She sat down on the top wooden step and I moved in front of her, knelt between her legs, the wood hard against my knees. Lucy leaned back on her elbows and tipped her head back to the snow. It fell on her face like feathers. A piece caught in her eyelash and melted on her eyelid.

"I want you," she whispered. She pulled me to her with her

legs, wrapping them around me. "Quick, before it starts snowing harder."

You don't forget something like that.

***

Lying next to her that night, listening to the sound of a cold wind sluicing around the corner of the house, I said to Lucy, "I think it'll be good to see everyone."

"I think so, too," she whispered.

CHAPTER THIRTY-ONE

The others started arriving at around noon the next day. Steve and Carla were the first to show, pulling into the snowy, unpaved driveway in Steve's blue Wrangler. She was driving, and before they even climbed out of the Jeep I could tell that their drive had been anything but pleasant.

"Look out," I whispered to Lucy, who was standing next to me, still wrapped in a blanket. She didn't reply, but just watched quietly as Steve and Carla grabbed bags from the bed of the truck and started toward the house, a healthy distance separating them. Lucy went to get dressed.

I worked hard to manufacture a smile and said, "Hey, guys. How was the trip?"

Carla half-dropped, half-tossed her duffle toward the door and muttered, "Just fucking swell." Performing a swift about face, she headed back toward the truck for another load.

"Some people you just can't make happy," Steve said, trying his best to smile. "Don't worry. She'll come around."

"What's the deal?" I asked.

Steve's eyes skipped around the room, and I could feel him looking for signs of what Lucy and I had been up to. "Nothing important," he said. With that, he hoisted his own bag and the one Carla had dropped near the front porch and hauled them into the house.

Jerome and a girl named Alice showed up about half-an-hour later. I knew Alice only peripherally, but one didn't need to know her well to form a solid idea of what she was about. Alice, whose last name was Stanton or Stevens or something along those lines, wore her convictions like clothing. She rarely failed to chime in on any topic, even if she wasn't involved in a particular conversation. I knew she had been involved in environmental protests while still in high school, and I'd heard rumors she'd even been detained for questioning by the police after a bomb threat was phoned in at Penton during her freshman year.

She and Jerome had seen each other a few times, but Jerome changed sexual partners with the frequency most people did underwear, so it hadn't occurred to me that Alice would actually show up to take part in Steve's film. I thought she'd be a good, hard-nosed person to have around for the next few days, though. It wasn't hard to imagine the shoot turning into a three day booze-fest, and I thought Alice would help to keep things moving.

I helped Jerome carry the bags up to one of the bedrooms and arrived back in the kitchen just in time to hear another car pull into the drive. I expected Dan, and with him was a girl named Megan, a tiny, pixyish blonde with enormous green eyes and an aura of the most country-bred innocence. I helped them both inside.

Steve was in the kitchen drinking a beer when I returned. "That's all of us," he said. "Hard to believe this is actually going to happen."

Us, I thought, and smiled at the thought of our little group. It's hard to believe how naïve I was.

***

That night we all gathered together in the living room, clustered around the hearth. As Lucy and I had discovered the night before, the furnace in the basement, while operational, struggled to keep the temperature in the house at a level one could define as warm, but the huge stone fireplace threw off enough heat to make up the difference.

Over enormous sandwiches Steve made, our conversation built and petered out and then built again, increasing in volume as we drank bottle after bottle of the beer. We would begin filming the next day.

"Hey, Paul," Steve said, prying the top off another bottle of beer with the butt end of a lighter. "Want to give these guys an overview?"

"Sure," I said, feeling an odd sense of embarrassment now that my story was about to be revealed. "But just remember, even Shakespeare sounds stupid in summary."

"Are you comparing yourself to Shakespeare?" Alice said.

I chuckled. "When you hear what this story is about, you'll realize just how insane that would be." And then I took them through it.

CHAPTER THIRTY-TWO

When I woke up the next morning at 5:30, I found Lucy in the kitchen reading the copy of the script I'd given her during our trip down. She looked up when I walked in and gave me a small smile, setting the script down on the table.

"Hi," I said, and kissed her.

She was quiet as I poured myself coffee and sat down beside her at the kitchen table.

"Everything okay?" I asked.

Looking down at the table, she said, "You wrote this, right?"

"Yeah, with Steve. It's from my story, though, the one I told you about that night at the Strand."

"Right, I remember."

She still hadn't looked at me, and I felt my stomach tighten. I moved closer to her. "Is there something wrong with it?"

"No," she said. "I was just surprised by some of what's in there, I guess. I'll be fine." She picked my hand up off the table and kissed the back of it. "Really. I don't know what's wrong with me. Come here."

I leaned in and kissed her. "Breakfast?" I asked.

"Absolutely."

***

Within hours of starting at seven that first morning at the Ballentemps farm, before the sun had even peeked over the mountains, we managed to film the initial three scenes of the movie, starting off with Steve and me, the two brothers, talking about their father's recent death, revealing to each other the horrible things to which each of them had been subjected. From there we moved on to the shot of Steve bolting from the room with a bottle of whiskey clutched in his hand, determined to leave the cabin.

Once we had that in the can, we shifted locations to the abandoned cabin Steve had noticed on the road as he and Carla had driven up the day before. Using the Super 8 camera Steve had borrowed from school, Lucy shot from the exterior as Steve barged out of the cabin and as I tailed him to the car and got in with him. Steve had also brought along a portable sound recorder, and because so many of the opening shots were static in location, we managed with no trouble to position the boom mike nearby and out of sight.

Before long, our process was set. Steve would set each shot and tell Lucy what he wanted to see. She would ask any questions, and then we'd go. By the time we were finished with the first two scenes, we had four or five takes of each, all from different angles.

For the interior car scenes Lucy filmed from the back seat, and then, just after I yelled out, "Watch out!" she moved to the edge of the steep slope on the side of the road and shot as the car went over the edge. Steve accomplished the accident scene by finding a place where the underbrush was sparse enough to allow the passage of the car's chassis. He piloted the vehicle gently down the brushy hill to the base of a big elm tree and nudged the hood up against the trunk. With a pot of boiling water that fumed angrily in the cold air, we created the illusion that steam was rushing from the engine, and filmed the two brothers climbing out of the car to inspect the damage, now stuck deep in

200

the woods with a ruined car.

Because it was cold and because we'd already gotten farther along than we'd expected to get on our first morning, we decided to break there until night and headed back to the farm.

"Some pretty cool stuff," Steve said to me and Lucy as we climbed into the car. "It's going to look great. I never thought it would go that smoothly."

"It was bizarre watching the two of you pretending to be other people all day," Lucy said, and laughed. "I can't believe how well it came off."

"You think so?" Steve said, glancing over at her.

Lucy nodded. "You two just *seemed* like brothers."

I glanced over at Steve and found him looking at me.

"Good news," he said, then started up the car.

When we got back to the barn, we found that Jerome and Dan had already done the clean-up work we'd decided to do that afternoon. The old building had been in rough shape...lengths of rotten wood lying scattered on the floor, old bales of hay slumped at odd intervals around the place, rusted equipment crowded into every conceivable place. In the few hours Steve, Lucy, and I had been gone, however, Steve's fraternity brothers had turned that mess into an atmospheric set.

Fresh hay that they'd picked up at a feed and supply store in Calderville was clumped here and there on the packed-dirt floor, and they had replaced the burnt-out light bulbs dangling from the ceiling on long, fraying wires with new, low-wattage bulbs that shed a dim yellow light.

"Damn, boys," Steve said.

I echoed the sentiment. I didn't know what I'd expected from Dan and Jerome, but it certainly wasn't this level of excitement and involvement. It made me feel like *part* of something.

Jerome, sweating from head to foot—it was cold outside, but it was hot and damp inside the barn—grunted and said, "We were just sitting around drinking."

"Wasn't just us, anyway," Dan added, wiping his forehead with the sleeve of his T-shirt. "Carla and Alice helped out with the hay."

"Where are those guys now?" I asked.

"Back in the house doing girl shit," Jerome said. "I kinda want to go watch."

Dan laughed and wiped sweat from his face with the back of a dirty hand, leaving a streak of brown across one cheek.

Steve looked at me. "We can start shooting in here tonight."

And so after a quick lunch of sandwiches and beer, Steve, Lucy, and I headed back out, this time with Jerome and Dan.

First we got the shot of the hillbillies picking us up from the site of our broken down car, then we quickly filmed the scene where all of us were in the truck together, the two brothers increasingly anxious as they realized that they weren't being taken toward any town, but somewhere much worse.

Happy with our work that day, we called it quits until darkness fell.

***

We'd been drinking all day. That's what I think about now, what I wish I'd paid attention to then. Even with those guys who could drink like that for weeks, it was a lot of beer and Jack Daniels, ever since we'd finished the afternoon shoot. There was a sodden, tired sense of purpose about everything we did.

"When we get through this," Steve said at one point, a cold beer in one hand, a cigarette in the other, "we're basically done. Just one last push." He sounded different than he had earlier in the day, eager not to get the next great shot, but eager to be *finished*. It should have worried me, but I was tired, too, and just wanted to be asleep upstairs with Lucy.

So we drank beer and whiskey and went through the motions. It was only once we'd gotten the two brothers into the barn that the trouble started, and what is still the hardest thing to accept is that all of the ugliness that followed could so easily have been avoided had I known just *one thing*. If I'd have been sensitive enough to understand why Lucy was drinking that day, why she was plowing through beer after beer, not slowing as the afternoon moved along, but picking up the pace. If I'd understood why Steve's mood darkened sharply as we neared shooting time for the last scene of the night. Had I known the reason, the secret, I could have done something.

But, as is so common, the worst things seem to result from the most basic misconceptions. I thought Lucy was trying to cope with being stuck together all day with me and Steve, and with what had happened at school with her father. And I thought Steve was preoccupied with filming. It would take far too long for me to find out the truth about what happened that night.

***

In a nutshell, the schedule for the nighttime session was to shoot three scenes. The first captured the two brothers being shoved into the barn, then panicking as the door was shut and locked behind them.

Because Steve and I were the only two actors in the scene with lines, it went easily, and it passed through my mind at one early point that I was starting to love something about acting. It was liberating to be someone else for a while, not to be bound by all the rules and morals I wrapped myself in everyday.

The trouble started as we were preparing for the next scene, a segment that would introduce the brothers to the other occupants of the barn, the women held captive in the stalls.

Carla and Alice were outfitted with loose-fitting flannel shirts and old jeans we'd rubbed down with dirt and torn in several places. Before long the costumes looked like garments the girls had been wearing for months on end. Steve and I finished off the costuming by smearing dirt on Carla and Alice's faces and

203

working a few pieces of hay into their mussed hair.

In preparation for the scene the girls took their places in the stalls, working themselves down in the piles of fresh hay Jerome and Jesse had supplied.

"Okay," Steve said, "this is where it gets weird. You need to lie there with your legs sort of spread, like you're waiting, okay?"

And that's when it all started.

CHAPTER THIRTY-THREE

We were just finishing up our walk-through of the scene when Steve suddenly stopped talking and looked up, a puzzled expression on his face.

"Do you hear that?" he said to no one in particular. I stopped adjusting the boom mike and listened. Far off, I heard a rumble.

"Car," I said, and realized that the sound was coming closer. I let go of the mike and walked to the barn door in time to see Roscoe's pickup come too fast out of the woods, bouncing like a toy over the unpaved road. The truck crested one last bump, bottomed out, then skidded to a stop near the rest of the parked cars.

The driver's side door of the truck opened and Roscoe climbed out, slammed the door behind him, and half-ran, half-walked toward the house.

I stepped out of the barn and yelled, "Roscoe, over here!"

He almost lost his balance on the icy top layer of snow, and then hurried in my direction. As he drew closer I could see his eyes were red and puffy, and it could be no secret that he'd been crying, and recently. He kept looking up and down and from side to side, over my shoulders, anywhere but into my eyes. I could practically feel the waves of energy coming off him, like heat from an oven when the door has been left open.

Roscoe started to say something, but his words caught in his throat and clicked dryly there. He coughed so violently that it bent him over.

Aware that the rest of the group had come out of the barn and were standing behind us, I said to Roscoe, "Let's get a beer."

As I took his arm and led him toward the house, I glanced back and met Lucy's eyes for a moment, hoping to communicate to her that I'd handle this for now, but what I saw in her face instead was a brand of confused distraction I had trouble reconciling. Her normally sharp eyes were glazed and looked not at me, but past me, at nothing.

I saw her sway slightly, and remembered how much she'd had to drink that day, so much more than I'd ever seen her drink before. Finally she realized I was looking at her and tipped her head in my direction, seeming to understand what I was trying to tell her.

As Roscoe and I walked away, I heard her tell the others to come back into the barn to continue setting up the next shot. She was slurring.

***

In the kitchen I took two beers from the icebox and popped the tops on the edge of the counter.

"Here," I said, handing Roscoe a bottle. "Give this a try."

Robotically, Roscoe closed his hand around the neck of the bottle, and when he did I could feel a powerful trembling thrumming through the glass. It reminded me of the way air sometimes felt back in Swarthmore during the summer just before a nasty thunderstorm.

Roscoe closed his eyes and took several deep breaths. When he opened them again some of the feverish intensity seemed to have gone from his body; his out-and-out shaking had diminished to a low tremor.

"My grandmother died," he said.

"I'm sorry." It wasn't surprising, though.

Roscoe raised his hand in a sort of half-wave and said, "We knew it was going to happen. She'd had these small strokes in the past few years, and then a huge one just before break. It was only a matter of time. She was a nice lady." Roscoe took a drink from his bottle, then looked at me. "You have any butts, Paco?"

I pulled a couple from the pack in my breast pocket, gave him one, and lit us both up. Roscoe took a long drag and held the smoke for a long beat before letting it go.

"I was there when she died," Roscoe said. "We all were, but my mom and dad weren't in the room. She'd gone to the cafeteria to get us all some coffee, and my dad...." Just mentioning the man seemed to shoot a pang of anguish straight through Roscoe. He took a breath and steadied himself. "My dad was outside smoking a cigarette. I was sitting in the hospital room next to the bed, and I saw this book on the bedside table. It was *The Adventures of Horatio Hornblower*. My grandma used to read it to me when I was a kid, but I hadn't thought about it in years. I don't know how it got there, but I think my mom might have brought it from home." Roscoe's eyes were bright with tears, and as I watched, they overflowed.

"It's okay," I said.

Roscoe shook his head. "It's so far from okay."

He drank from his beer, finished it, then set the bottle on the kitchen table. "Anyway, she died. I wanted to read some dumb book to her, and she died, and when my dad came in, he said, 'finally.'"

I felt helpless. There was nothing to say to that. "Bastard," I said.

"Yeah. Bastard. It's what I said too, only in the hospital room, only in front of his wife and some pretty nurses."

It was then that I saw the bruises on Roscoe's neck. Slender, shaped like fingers.

"I must have blacked out for a while," Roscoe said. His eyes had grown far-away. "The next thing I knew I was standing in the living room, and I had the poker from the fireplace in my hand."

My stomach flipped and I suddenly felt my heart in my throat. I wanted him to stop talking. "You didn't—"

Roscoe waved me off. "No," he said, "but I could have, if I'd wanted to. All I did was poke him in the shoulder with it to wake him up, and when he opened his eyes, I said that if he ever tried to hit me again, I'd kill him. And then I got in the car and came here."

"This is where you belong."

But it wasn't really. This was Roscoe's parents' house, dirty and neglected, and I had no idea what memories it held for him, good or bad. I felt pulled back to the barn then, to ward off whatever had come over Lucy, to see what had happened to my script, and I felt pulled to my role in this kitchen with Roscoe. I felt, for the first time, like an adult, like I feel now when I feel too old for my skin. Overburdened. Overwhelmed.

"Go back to the shooting," Roscoe said. "They need you out there."

"Yeah," I said. "Okay." And I stood to go.

It's amazing what you can miss when you're not looking for it. I'll think about my choice to leave him there, sitting alone in the kitchen, for the rest of my life.

CHAPTER THIRTY-FOUR

When I got back to the barn set I found that Steve had finished prepping the shot. He and Lucy were standing together near the back of the barn, talking. Steve said something, a pained look on his face, and Lucy slashed at the air with her hands, and then she saw me.

She turned to Jerome, lifted the camera to her shoulder, and said, "Are you guys ready?" The far away look I'd seen in her eyes just before I took Roscoe inside was gone, but she looked agitated, her movements jerky and almost uncoordinated. What the hell had she and Steve been talking about? An image of her sitting in the kitchen reading the script that morning flashed through my mind, and then was gone before I knew where it had come from.

"Luce," I said quietly, "can we talk?" Her eyes twitched in my direction and I knew she'd heard me, but she didn't respond, and the others seemed oblivious to what was happening with her.

"Yup." Jerome flicked a switch on the boom mike and lifted it above all of our heads. "Let's get it on."

"Places," Lucy said, her voice unsteady, and I understood that if we were going to talk at all, it would be when we were finished with the two scenes. *Fifteen minutes*, I told myself. *If we don't mess around, we can have this thing in the can in fifteen minutes, maybe less.*

"Everyone ready?" Lucy asked. Her voice sounded more uncertain now than ever. I wanted to ask her if she was okay, but there were people around, and I told myself we only had a few more minutes left before we could stop for the night. After the take I would talk to her. I nodded to her and saw Steve and Carla do the same.

"Ready," Steve said.

Lucy put her eye to the camera and said, "Action," dropping her hand in a signal that said: go.

Jerome's arm tightened around me and I felt the rubbery blade of the knife press against my throat. "Get in there," he growled at Steve. "You got ten seconds and then this one's dead."

Steve looked to me, an entirely convincing look of unsure panic in his eyes.

"I don't want to die," I said, reciting the line with as much conviction as I could muster, trying hard to resist the urge to look over at Lucy to see how she was doing.

"I don't know if I can," Steve said, a quaver vibrating in his voice.

Jerome jabbed the fake knife even deeper into my neck and growled, "I'll slice him open from ear to ear." For emphasis he tightened the arm around my chest. I felt the air whistling out of my lungs as he did. If he got any more enthusiastic, I was going to be in trouble. "Get in there," Jerome added, taking the knife from my neck for long enough to gesture at the stall where Carla waited.

Steve took a tentative step toward the stall.

"That's it," Jerome said. "Go on."

Out of the corner of my eyes I saw Lucy. Her face was pale, and the camera was shaking perceptibly on her shoulder. The feeling that something was terribly wrong swept over me, but I knew that if she could just hold it together for a couple of more minutes, we'd be done and I could talk first to her and then to Roscoe. Just a little longer.

And then I knew what was wrong. It came to me all at once, a flash of understanding, of connection.

Suddenly I wasn't in the barn anymore, but back in Penton on Spring Street, walking hand-in-hand with Lucy on a snowy night.

I was raped, I heard her say, heard her say it quickly and uncertainly, as though I might let go of her hand in disgust and walk away. How had I missed it, failed to make the connection between what had happened to her and what I was asking her to film?

I had to stop this.

In front of me Steve edged toward the stall and stopped at the door. He looked unsure, distracted. I looked over at Lucy and saw tears sliding down her cheeks, but the camera was trained steadily on Steve.

Jerome said, "There you go. Get to it, boy."

After a brief pause, Steve's hands moved jerkily to his belt and he fumbled it open. When he spoke, his voice was flat and robotic. "I don't want to do this. I can't."

"Stop," I said, my voice strange and strained under the pressure of Jerome's knife. "Don't."

"Don't," I said again to Steve, trying to jerk myself free of Jerome's hard grasp, but he pulled me back tightly against his chest, his arm tight on my neck. I couldn't think of what to say to make it stop, what the word was that would turn us back into ourselves. "Don't, man. Stop it. We can't do this."

Steve looked back at me, and I saw an expression on his face of fear and disgust that I couldn't believe was just acting. Then I realized that it *wasn't* acting; he had just come to the same

211

realization I had, that the two of us had set Lucy up to see the worst experience of her life reenacted.

Steve dropped to his knees in front of Carla, and I found Lucy again in my peripheral vision.

I watched as the camera slowly dropped from her shoulder. It dangled from her hand for a moment before she let it go. It thumped on the hay littering the floor, still running.

"Stop," I said as Steve moved on top of Carla, and when no one reacted, I screamed, "Stop the fucking scene!" This time I got free of Jerome, but Lucy was already headed for the door of the barn. I put my hand on her arm.

"Lucy, wait."

When she turned to me there was nothing in her face I recognized. I didn't have time to raise my hands before her open hand hit me hard on the side of the head, clapping my ear, knocking me to the side. I stumbled and went down on one knee, then got back up to go after her, but she wasn't in the barn anymore.

I put my hand to where Lucy had hit me, gaping at the open doorway, wondering what to do.

"Don't go after her," Alice said. "Leave her alone."

She was right, I knew. There's no way I'd be able to talk to her now, and maybe not ever again. She hadn't read the script when I gave it to her. She hadn't known this was the story from the first. I realized now she thought I was telling *her* story, the thing she hadn't had the courage to tell another soul, and I was putting it on film.

An ugly black shame leaked into my chest. Something had to be wrong with me not to see it before. The courage it must have taken to tell me in the first place, to walk me through it, and then for me to disregard her privacy. I felt like a monster. I wanted nothing more than to talk to her, to find her and hold her and tell her I hadn't thought, just *hadn't seen it*.

Something suddenly glimmered in my brain and I turned around. "Where's Steve?" I said.

Jerome, who was sitting on a bale of hay drinking from a bottle of beer, said, "Think he went out the back."

Dan came into the barn through the front door and found me. "She's in the house. I saw a light go on upstairs." He put his hand on my back, squeezed my shoulder. "It'll blow over, man."

"Paul," Alice said. "Not yet. Okay?"

"I won't," I said. I was going to find Steve first. I couldn't get out of my head the bizarre way both he and Lucy had acted during the shoot. He had some kind of role in all of this, and I wanted to know what it was.

Chapter Thirty-Five

As I stepped outside into the woody area behind the barn, the cold air slapped hard at my face. I wasn't wearing a coat, and the wind had kicked up. It now had a moist cutting edge to it, and I could smell snow coming.

Ahead of me a narrow trail cut into the woods and I plunged down it, my arms held up to block branches. In my skull a thousand thoughts swarmed like angry bees, but I could make no sense of them. One would stop for half a second in the front of my brain and I would grasp at it, then it would be gone again, leaving me with only a ghostlike impression that something important was there, if only I could see it.

A thin branch snapped at my face, making my eyes water. I swung blindly at the darkness and felt a sob of frustration and confusion welling in my chest.

Steve's voice stopped me. "Paul."

I swiveled my head to both sides, looking for him, saw a red glow in the darkness a few feet ahead of me, and angled toward it.

Steve had stopped in a small natural clearing in the trees. Filtered moonlight lit the rocky, frozen ground, and I saw that Steve was sitting on a stump, smoking. I could see the cigarette shaking in his hand.

"Why didn't you say something?" I demanded, feeling frustration and anger bubbling through my veins. "You *had* to know that would happen! That something would happen!"

His head whipped around to me. "I *did* say something to her, you fucking asshole! I talked to her about it this afternoon, and you know what? I expected her to know already. *Jesus*, Paul! Why do you think she's been drinking so much? She wanted to go through with it for you, so she wouldn't let you down!" He glared at me and shook his head in disgust. "All you had to do was let her read the script. She wouldn't have gotten involved."

I stepped toward him, feeling my pulse in my temples. "I didn't even know about what happened to her until yesterday. Fuck!"

Steve leaned even closer to me. "I took care of her. You were supposed to do that now. You fucked up. You should have left her alone."

From a place beyond conscious thought I heard a voice telling me to stop, but my body was acting on its own. I grabbed Steve's shirt and shoved him backwards, let go, punched at him, and felt my fist connect with the side of his head. He cried out and fell to the ground and I pounced on him, swinging my hands at his head, making only sporadic and glancing contact. And then I had no breath and he was on top of me, screaming and punching. I felt his fingernails rip across my cheek and a blaze of pain.

Then he stopped, and I quickly realized why.

"Do you smell that?" Steve whispered, pushing to his knees.

"Smoke," I said.

CHAPTER THIRTY-SIX

The curtains in the living room had been pulled open and tucked into the cloth loops that held them that way, so my view of the living room was unobstructed. It passed through my mind quickly and uselessly that I'd never noticed that the drapes were parted, and if they'd been that way since Lucy and I first arrived at the farm, anyone could have seen us through the window as we made love on the couch that first night.

As I watched a tongue of fire snaked out and ignited a bowl of pine cones sitting on the mantel. A trail of fire climbed the wall on the fire side of the room, and I saw the white paint scorch, the fire spreading across the ceiling like a spilled drink. Sparks burst from the light fixture in the middle of the room, and then the light flickered once and the bulb exploded.

Okay, a voice in my mind said. *Go in there.*

And so I did.

***

I heard glass shatter from somewhere deeper inside the house, once, then twice, and then three times as window after window blew out from the heat.

The stairs were on fire. Not just the banister, which had already blackened and now oozed flame only from its rounded

216

top, like a match burning in reverse, but also the brown shag carpet that lined the staircase. The carpet fibers hissed and spit, and in places where it had completely burned away, I saw charred wood starting to ignite. If I managed to get up to the second story at all, I'd burn my legs badly, and that still left me the trip back down with Lucy.

There was no way. No way. And then I remembered the ladder. Outside, leaning against the side of the barn.

My eyes burning, I headed back to the stairs and pulled the door open, stepping outside into the crystalline air.

Roscoe, who was sitting Indian-style on the frozen ground, looked up at me with an expression of abject confusion and said, "What the hell are you doing?"

"The house is burning!" I screamed at him, my voice dry and raspy from the smoke and heat. "Can't you see that?!"

"Of course I can," he said.

And then I saw the baggage littering the ground behind him—my bags, Lucy's, Steve's, *everyone's*—and understood.

"You did this," I said, reeling. "You started it."

Roscoe smiled. "Had to do something, you know? Don't worry, though. All your shit's out here. All of it is. Got every last bag. You can—"

"Lucy's in there!" I screamed.

CHAPTER THIRTY-SEVEN

There are brief flashes I remember between the time I blacked out in the burning house and when I woke up a day and a half later in a hospital bed. I remember prying open a second floor window and entering the house. I remember the sound of Roscoe's skin sizzling on a brass doorknob, though I couldn't recall where in the house we had been, or why Roscoe was with me; I knew I'd gone in alone. I remember a bloody handprint on a white T-shirt. My right hand was badly gashed from the wrist to the webbing between my first two fingers, so I thought the handprint may have been mine, the T-shirt Lucy's.

I remember lying on the icy ground, my head on someone's lap, seeing Roscoe beside me, the clothing almost completely burned from his body, smoke rising from his skin and hair, much of which had been burned away. I didn't see Lucy, or if I did, I don't remember seeing her then.

Alice hovered over me, and she was wrapping something around my wrist and hand and crying, telling me it was going to be okay.

I also don't remember being burned, but I was. My hands would spend the next several weeks shedding layers of ruined skin, and the scars would always be there.

I remember the sound of an ambulance arriving, sirens wailing, being jolted into the back of it, lying next to someone, realizing it was Steve, his clothing blackened, the sleeves of his shirt burned completely away in places, his hands red and blistered. I remember thinking, *but Steve wasn't in the house.*

And then I woke up, and I found out how bad it all really was, and that nothing would ever be the same again.

***

The doctor who came in to talk to me that morning broke the news to me gently. He sat in a chair beside my bed and patted my leg sympathetically as I cried, and told me I was going to be fine, just fine in no time. When I put my hand through the window, he told me, I'd lacerated my hand badly and nicked an artery in my wrist. If Alice hadn't bandaged me as I lay in the snow, I could very easily have bled to death, but I hadn't hurt myself in a way that would have lasting effects. Roscoe, he said, had been very badly burned and had been transferred to a hospital in Memphis that could better care for his injuries. Steve was in another room across from mine, and I could see him later that day if I wanted.

When I asked about Lucy, however, the doctor was quiet for a long moment. When he finally spoke, he did so with the look of a man who was doing something he knew he shouldn't. Lucy, he said, had died of smoke inhalation. Her lungs had simply been overwhelmed, and she'd drowned in smoke lying in bed. Because she had been drunk and unconscious already, there would have been no pain. It was Roscoe who had carried Lucy from the house, and then he'd come back for me. He had managed to drag me as far as the kitchen before collapsing, and it was Steve who had found us there and hauled our limp bodies from the flames.

The doctor asked me if he could get me anything, if I was in pain. I told him that I would be fine, and when he left a few minutes later for rounds, I removed the IV drip from my arm, climbed out of bed, and went looking for Lucy.

219

A nurse found me calling her name as I walked up and down the hallway, opening doors to look inside. Blood leaked from my mouth because I'd reopened the wounds in my throat. I was taken back to bed and sedated.

When I woke up in the morning I was overwhelmed, and I cried as hard and as long as I ever would. My doctor seemed to be reassured by my emotional outpouring, and told the nurses to do away with my restraints.

That afternoon I went next door and visited Steve.

***

His arms and hands were burned, and like mine they were wrapped in thick wads of gauze. He lay still in bed, arms crossed over his stomach, looking out the window at the bright winter day outside.

"Steve," I said.

His head jerked around as if I'd been about to strike him.

"Hey, it's just me, man," I said, holding my hands up. "You all right?"

He curled his body into the fetal position and covered his face with his padded hands, and his body started to hitch. A wrenching sob ripped its way free of his chest, and I heard footsteps clattering down the hallway toward the room.

I moved closer to the bed, wanting to comfort Steve, and got halfway there just as the door burst open behind me. A nurse rushed in, brushing by me. She leaned over Steve and turned back to look at me, a scowl on her face.

"What happened?" she said. "He was fine before."

"I don't know," I answered. "I just came in."

"Well, leave then," she snapped. "Try again tomorrow. Maybe he'll have calmed down by then."

I backed toward the door, watching as the nurse took a needle from her apron and jabbed it into Steve's arm. He stopped wailing and turned onto his back.

As I gripped the door handle behind me, Steve's voice stopped me. "Paul," he said.

Holding the door half-open, I turned back toward him. "Yeah?"

He choked back another sob, his face wet with tears. "It's my fault, man. I killed her."

His words made no sense to me then, and I'd soon forget about them in that way people do when they're fighting to maintain their grip on the world. I already had enough; I didn't want anything else.

***

The next day my parents arrived from Pennsylvania, and they took shifts sitting with me in my room while the other slept for a few hours at a hotel a few miles down the road.

On Sunday they took me out of the hospital and we flew home.

CHAPTER THIRTY-EIGHT

I reached Cincinnati at around four o'clock in the afternoon, and I found myself reeling. Nine hours ago I'd woken up in my own bed in Wallingford, concerned about an old friend. Now I was in Ohio, hundreds of miles away from my wife and my daughter and the rest of the normal life I'd made for myself. Where I was going I'd never been. Once, when I was eighteen years old, I had been in love with a girl who had grown up there, and it was the one place she'd never wanted to return to.

As I followed signs toward Danbury, I switched on my cell phone and dialed Dottie's number. She answered on the first ring.

"Where are you?" she said.

"This is going to sound crazy," I said, "so don't freak out. I'm in Ohio."

There was silence on the other end of the line for a long moment, and then Dottie said, "Okay. Can I ask you *why* you're in Ohio, Paul?"

"You know how I met my friend Steve for a drink last night?" I asked.

"Sure. Your friend from college."

"Right. Well, when I woke up this morning, something was bugging me about the things he said. No, that's not right.

Something was bugging me about the things he *didn't* say, and I thought that maybe he was trying to get me to talk him out of doing something to hurt himself."

"So you decided to go to Ohio to talk him out of it."

I almost told her about my visit with Roscoe and then reconsidered. Although I was a little disoriented by my own actions during the course of the day, I was still aware that my activities would seem twice as strange to someone not fully aware of all the details. "That's the long and short of it," I said. Lying wasn't something I did, and it made me feel dirty.

As I waited for her to respond, I could picture her face in my mind. Her eyes would be closed, and she would be taking long, silent breaths to calm herself down. It was unfair that I was putting her through this, that I'd been putting her through this in one way or another for the entirety of our marriage, but Dottie knew what I was. And although she didn't know *all* of my history, she knew enough to understand that there were some things I'd always be working to resolve.

"Paul," she finally said, "do you know when you'll be home?"

"Tonight," I said. "Tomorrow morning at the latest. I'm just going to go by Steve's place and see what can be done, if anything."

"Call me later and let me know you're okay."

"I will," I said. "I love you. Thank you for understanding."

"I didn't say I understand. Call me soon."

We hung up and I stopped at a gas station and bought a map of Ohio. In ten minutes I was back on the road, heading for Danbury.

CHAPTER THIRTY-NINE

When I arrived in town, I stopped at a gas station and asked where I could find Walnut Lane.

"That's big money country," the attendant said. He was a large man of about sixty with ruddy red cheeks who looked like he'd be able to recite the history of every person in the town if you'd only ask.

"Is that right?" I said. "A friend of mine lives there, but I've never been."

"Well, it's easy enough to find. Just head out onto Pressman, turn left on Third, and then look for the entrance to the school. That's Walnut."

"Walnut's on the Grimwald campus?" When Steve had called yesterday, he had told me he was in Philadelphia for an academic convention. A lie, but one close to the truth. He was a teacher, or something along those lines. At the very school where he and Lucy had gone, no less, the place where her life had been set by a human monster on a sad and tragic track.

I thanked him and got back into the car, thinking that maybe I was starting to understand. This town had always linked Steve and Lucy; both had kept secret from me and from everyone else the history they shared here. I thought maybe there was a reason for that, and that I might now know what that reason was.

After Lucy was raped, she had forced herself onto a boy from her high school. Those had been her words, and her reticence about saying anything more specific should have been as telling to me then as it was now.

I had no doubt that boy had been Steve.

***

A quarter of a mile after I turned onto Third Street, I saw a gray stone gate on the right, with the words GRIMWALD SCHOOL etched into each of the side columns, and turned through it.

Immediately the landscape changed. Where the rest of Danbury was small-town Ohio, Grimwald was a different world.

Enormous oak trees with leafless limbs reached across the road toward each other and out over the manicured lawns that fronted the stately houses beyond. It reminded me of the nicest parts of the Main Line in Philadelphia, towns where the parents were invariably doctors and lawyers, and where their children wore privilege like it didn't cost a thing. This was the kind of place where they didn't like trouble unless it was over money. I couldn't imagine Lucy or Steve growing up here.

Steve's house was as large as the rest on Walnut Lane, but there was no denying that its upkeep had been neglected over the years. On one side, a gutter sagged at a gentle angle from the flat roof. The lawn itself told the same story; through the thin layer of icy snow that crusted the dead grass, I could see a trellis that had collapsed under the weight of whatever it had supported, and which now lay propped just off the ground on a rotting log.

I wondered what I was here to do. Dottie had asked me that very question on the phone not long ago, and I'd offered her a bogus answer, one that sounded good to me at the time, but which meant nothing. Was I expecting some kind of absolution from Steve, a release from the guilt that had followed me all these years? I thought so, and there was something rotten about that. If

225

it was Steve's fault, if he truly believed that he had been the one who drove Lucy from the barn and into the house that night, then it couldn't be *my* fault, could it?

I knocked, and after a few seconds I heard footsteps approaching, then the door opened and I found myself standing face to face with my old friend for the second time in two days.

"How'd you find out where I live?" Steve asked.

"It wasn't hard."

He stepped back out of the doorway and gestured with one arm for me to come inside. "Come on in."

I followed Steve into his kitchen, a large room wallpapered with a brown and maroon flower print that had probably been in style about thirty years ago. A lamp hanging from the ceiling lit the space, but only barely. In the sink I could see dirty dishes, and there was a smell in the air of rotting vegetables. A half-empty bottle of Jack Daniels and a tumbler sat on a table in the breakfast area.

"Not too good, is it?" Steve said, as if reading my thoughts. He smiled thinly. "It used to be a great house when I was a kid. My father's pride and joy. But that was a long time ago. Drink?"

"Sure," I said, sitting down at the round table.

Steve took a glass from a cabinet and poured a generous portion of Jack Daniels into it, then put it down in front of me and sat in the chair opposite mine. He produced a pack of cigarettes from his breast pocket and tapped one out and lit it, exhaling the smoke slowly so that it drifted up over his face.

"So, what brings you?" he said, an ironic grin tilting the corners of his mouth.

"I was worried about you."

He laughed softly. "Worried about me," he repeated, more to himself than anything. "That's a good one. Worried that I might do what, kill myself or something?"

I shrugged. "Maybe. I don't know. Is that something you've

thought about?"

For a moment he didn't answer, then he said, "Not in a long time, Paul. Not in a very long time."

"Good," I said. Feeling emboldened, I added, "I went to see Roscoe earlier today. He said you were there a couple of days ago."

"He really got the short end, didn't he?"

"When was the last time you'd seen him?"

"A few months after the...." Steve seemed to struggle to choose a word, then finally said, "after the fire. I wanted to talk to him about what had happened, but he was still in so much pain and they had him pretty drugged up. I don't know if he heard anything I said."

"What did you want to tell him?"

Steve shrugged, inhaled smoke. "That what happened wasn't his fault. He'd been through enough. I knew he blamed himself."

"He set the fire," I said.

"Yeah," Steve said, "but none of that would have mattered if Lucy wasn't in the house. Everything would be different if she'd just stayed in the barn, or if she'd never been there in the first place."

I nodded slowly, not agreeing with Steve, just acknowledging that I'd heard what he said.

"Hey," Steve said softly, "do you remember what I said to you just before we realized the house was on fire?"

I thought back. "You told me I should have been looking out for Lucy. You said it was my turn to keep her safe, and that I fucked it up."

Steve shook his head. "It wasn't your fault. It was always mine. She told you about what happened to her in high school?"

"Yeah, the night before we got to the farm."

"I was a year older than she was, had known her since we were just kids. We grew up a couple of streets apart; her dad was the head of the upper school, mine was a teacher in the math department. I can't remember a time when I didn't have feelings of one kind or another for her."

"She didn't tell me you'd known each other for so long."

"I'm not surprised. I don't think our history was a subject she liked to rehash for anyone, even herself."

"Why not?"

"It's complicated." He closed his eyes, and when he opened them a moment later I knew he would continue. "I always loved her, but Lucy was never interested in being anything other than my friend. Still, some things you can't control, you know?"

"Sure."

He regarded me skeptically for a second, as though trying to decide whether I was being sincere. The moment passed and he went on.

"Winter of my senior year, I heard a guy talking in the locker room about what he'd done to a girl at a party. At first I didn't know he was talking about Lucy, but then I heard her name and I...I guess the only way to describe it is to say I lost my mind. I beat him within an inch of his life. I broke his arm and three of his ribs and his nose. Slammed his head right into a bench. I can still remember the sound his nose made when it went. His friends had no idea what to do with me. I also broke bones in both of my hands, but I didn't even realize it until I got home. He didn't come back to school for a couple of weeks."

"Jesus Christ." It was hard to imagine the Steve I knew in a frenzy of such anger and violence, but then I thought of what love could make a person do. I thought of Dottie, of Naomi. What if someone hurt my wife, my daughter? There were no words to say how far I would go.

"One of my finer moments," Steve said, and took a drag from his cigarette. "To top it off, I planted a dime bag of pot in his locker later that year, and then reported him to the dean. Even his daddy couldn't save him from that one."

We both laughed grimly and shook our heads, sipping from our drinks.

Steve continued. "So a few weeks after my little confrontation, Lucy showed up at my house while my parents were still at work and told me she knew what I did, and she thanked me, said no one else had done anything. She said her mom and dad knew, but they wouldn't go to the police, or to the boy's family. She was acting strange, and she wanted to go upstairs to my room. She didn't seem like she felt well, but she told me that she knew how I felt about her, said she wanted to...." He looked like he was going to be sick and stopped for a moment and put his hand to his mouth. I realized he was trying to hold back tears. "She said she wanted to say thank you."

"And she got pregnant."

"Yeah. The guy who did her abortion was a hack and screwed up her uterus so she couldn't ever have babies. At first I don't think Lucy cared, but after that she kept on getting darker and darker. She told me she couldn't be with me. It just made her think about all the bad things that had happened to her. So I was just her friend again. I went to Penton, and then she showed up the next year."

"Because she trusted you," I said.

He nodded. "I think so. There was no one else who ever stood up for her."

I swirled my drink around in the glass. "And you blame yourself for her death? Because you should have been there for her."

"You loved her. I know that. But you didn't know enough, not like I did. I wanted everything to be your fault or Roscoe's, anyone's, but as soon as it was over I knew that was bullshit. I knew being in that barn, shooting that scene with her there, all of it, might bring everything back for her. But I didn't say anything

229

until it was too late, until she'd already decided she was going to do it." Steve lit another cigarette and, almost as an afterthought, held the pack up toward me. I hadn't smoked a cigarette in more years than I could remember, but being there with Steve and the taste of the bourbon made me want one. I took it and Steve slid the lighter across the table to me.

"Because she might blame me for not stopping it?" I asked.

"Stupid, I know. But yeah, maybe. It wasn't anything I ever actually *thought* about, you know? I just *did* it." As I lit the cigarette he'd given me, Steve said, "I had my reasons for not telling you all of this before, you know."

"Like?"

"She loved you. You had what I'd always wanted. It was too hard for me. If she was alive, you'd still be together." He spoke deliberately, choosing each word with painful care. I felt his last statement sticking in my heart. "I was in two places, Paul. I loved you too, man. I knew it wasn't your fault, none of it. I wanted to talk about it, but...."

When he didn't finish, I said, "Why now, then? You came to Philadelphia to tell me all of this, right?"

Steve locked his eyes on mine. "I did, but then you started talking about your wife and your kid. It just seemed like you'd moved on, like you got out on the other side. I didn't want to pull you back in. I wish I'd never come, Paul. I mean that. It was...it was fucking selfish."

"Well, I'm back in," I said, holding up my hands. "So maybe answer the question, okay? Why now?"

Steve shrugged. "I'm going to die soon."

Since meeting Steve at the bar last night I'd suspected that something might be wrong with his health, but the words still stole my breath. "Why?"

He held up his cigarette. "Cancer. Maybe six months, maybe not."

"I'm so sorry, man."

He shook his head. "Like I've been saying, Paco, it's not your fault. You have nothing to apologize for."

I put my hand on his wrist. "I believe you. Now listen to me. Neither do you."

CHAPTER FORTY

It was easier than I'd thought it would be to find the house Lucy grew up in. Steve had given me directions, and like he said, the house was just a few streets over. Danbury wasn't a very big town; it was the kind of place where everyone would know everyone else's business. What must it have been like for Lucy here, after the rape, after the abortion, after her parents and everyone else knew what had happened to her? This was the kind of town that brought out the best and worst from its people. If someone got hurt or lost a child or a spouse, this was the town where that person could expect his neighbors to bring dinners by until he was back on his feet. It was also the place where, if there was the slightest whiff of scandal, a woman's neighbors would eat her alive.

For a few minutes I just sat in the car, letting the engine run and watching tiny flurries drift down to the lawn in front of the house, everything highlighted by the headlights. Eventually I got out of the car.

I rang the doorbell, and when no one came immediately, I rang it again, and then again. Finally I heard footsteps behind the door, then the lock clicked and the door swung slowly open.

When I'd first met him Lucy's father had been, by my own

estimation, somewhere in his mid forties. That would put him in his sixties now, and he looked older than that. He was dressed in a frayed brown bathrobe, and his shoulders were stooped with time and tiredness. He squinted at me from behind tortoise-shell glasses, and I noticed the way his thin wispy hair was pressed against the side of his head. There was no doubt in my mind that my knock had woken him from a sound slumber. I smelled something familiar in the air between us, and then realized what it was: scotch.

A black hole of memory sucked me down, and suddenly I was standing in the doorway of Lucy's dorm room, staring at the dark-haired man from whom alcohol-stench radiated in humid waves. I saw the spittle on his chin, the bulge of his eyes, felt the dull hum of pain in the back of my head where it had connected with the frame of Lucy's bed.

I hadn't known what I would feel when and if I ever came face to face with this man again, but now I found out.

There *was* anger, yes. And there was a bone-wearying sadness in my heart that felt like it would drag me to the ground. But standing in front of this monster who had, for all intents and purposes, sold his fifteen-year-old daughter's life for the price of a promotion, I felt *powerful*. It wasn't something I'd expected, but suddenly I felt within me the pain and sadness and suffering this man had caused in all of us...Lucy, me, Roscoe, and Steve. In all of the people we could have loved as they deserved. This man had destroyed lives. He had broken his own child and sent her out into the world on her own, where she had met Steve, and then me, two confused children ourselves, hardly prepared to take care of ourselves, much less someone else.

In front of this man now, I felt the need to do something, to say something that would convey every bit of what I was feeling, not just on my own behalf, but also for Lucy and Steve and Roscoe. Then the air went out of me and my shoulders slumped,

233

my neck suddenly too tired to hold my head. I knew all of that was impossible. It wasn't even necessary.

I understood that I didn't need to do anything more than leave this burden in the place where it truly belonged.

"Do you know who I am?" I said, holding my face in the light where Lucy's father would be able to see it clearly.

He shuffled a step closer to me and craned his neck forward, but I saw no recognition in his eyes.

"Paul Callahan," I said.

The old man raised a finger and pointed it at me. "You're the one who killed my daughter. Get off my property." He started to close the door, but I put my hand on it and pushed it open again.

"Don't you run away from me, old man," I said. "You stand there and listen to what I have to say."

He waved a hand in the air dismissively but stayed where he was, his hand still on the door, ready to close it as soon as I backed off. There were so many things I wanted to say, that I could *imagine* saying, but none of them would do justice to the enormity of what I wanted to express.

"You deserve to die alone," I said, then pulled the door closed behind me. I got back into my car and headed for Philadelphia.

CHAPTER FORTY-ONE

How do you say goodbye?

It was a question I found myself thinking about often in the days after I got back from Ohio, and I had the time and space to give it my full attention. Dottie was distant with me, and I could understand why. When I got home early the next morning, she was sitting in the living room, waiting.

"I love you," I told her.

"I believe you," she said. "But you've been holding out on me, Paul. For a long time. I didn't wait up because I wanted to yell at you. I just wanted to let you know that I deserve better than you've given me. I'm going to bed now. Think about what you want. I'm ready to talk when you are."

My head dropped in shame. If she'd always suspected there might be things about me she didn't know, those suspicions had been confirmed now. It was a fact I'd have to correct, and as much as I wanted to level with my wife, I dreaded the act of telling her, too.

The day after I got home, I went to work as usual and sat in my office, half-heartedly proofreading articles for the next edition of the magazine and responding to the emails that had cropped up in my inbox. Finally it was five and I got in my car to go home. I sat there, the engine running. Half an hour later, I put the car in drive, a different destination in mind.

***

The house where Nathan Greene lived was a few blocks from ours on a pleasant, sun-dappled street called Avondale. I pulled the car to the curb and climbed out. Nathan answered the door.

"Hey, Nathan," I said, smiling. I knew this had to look strange—hell, it *was* strange—and I didn't want him to feel threatened by me.

"Hey, Mr. Callahan. What's going on?" He was still standing behind the screen door.

"Can you come out for a sec, so we can talk?"

He hesitated, looking back over his shoulder. "Uh, sure, okay."

I leaned against the porch railing and crossed my arms, then uncrossed them when I realized what I was doing; "putting up barriers," as Dottie always said.

"Look," I said. "This is going to sound funny, but I just wanted to come by and let you know I don't have a problem with you. I know you're a good kid. I've been tough on you and I shouldn't have been. You haven't done anything wrong."

Nathan shifted uncomfortably from one foot to the other. "You've been a little tough, I guess."

"I know. Anyway, what I'm doing here is this. I wanted to ask if you'd come by our place for dinner tonight."

"Seriously?"

I shrugged. "Naomi's going to be pissed I'm doing this, but what can you do? Yeah, if you have the time, come by around seven, okay? We'll get pizza or something. That sound good?"

"Sure," he said. "Thanks."

I nodded at him and trotted down the stairs, feeling absurdly good and embarrassed, all at the same time.

***

After dinner I poured both Dottie and myself a glass of the Cakebread Cellars Zin we'd been saving. For a winter night it was comfortable, and Naomi and Nathan had walked into town to see a movie. We sat on the back deck in Adirondack chairs, lit only by the bright moon above.

"So, that was special," she said, and laughed. She wore white gloves and a puffy goose-down vest that I thought probably belonged to Naomi. "What, you just knocked on his door and asked him to come over for dinner?"

I laughed too. "Pretty much. Felt a little dirty, like I was asking him on a date or something. Was Naomi freaked out?"

"At first," Dottie said. "But…it just took her a while. It was a really sweet thing to do."

"Okay," I said. "I feel better now."

"Can I ask you *why* you felt compelled to do it?"

"Hard to say. I know I've been an ass. Maybe I just wanted to make up for it. Start, anyway."

"Okay," Dottie said, swishing wine around in her glass. She looked around the empty deck and yard, then back at me, smiling. "We're all alone out here. Did you plan this out so we could chat?"

"You've always been patient with me," I told her. "If you're ready to listen now, I'm ready to talk. It's going to be a lot more than you're expecting, and it might take a while."

"Okay," she said, sitting back, her glass of wine cradled in both hands. There was no hesitation in her voice or in her eyes. She was my person; she loved me. There was nothing I could tell her that would change that. I felt undeservedly blessed, and I vowed inside my own head never to take that for granted again.

"Go ahead," she said. "Tell me."

So I did.

***

When Steve died in May, I went to the funeral and took Dottie

237

with me. Roscoe was there, which surprised me. He was dressed in a crisp, black suit. Joanna, his helper, stood behind him and handed him a handkerchief when he started to cry from the eye the fire had spared.

Afterwards, I walked with them back to the van in which they'd driven from New York.

"I'd glad you came, Roscoe," I said as we walked. "I know Steve would have been, too." I paused, then added, "Maybe sometime you'll come to Philly, spend a couple of nights with me and the family."

He sucked oxygen from his mask. "Maybe. As long as you have TV and scotch."

I patted him on the shoulder, then squatted down in front of him and locked his eyes with my own. "If there's ever anything I can do, you'll let me know. And about that visit, I'll be waiting for a call."

"Sure," he said, and in his eyes I saw some of the old Roscoe. "Sure I will, Paco."

***

As I lay in bed awake that night, my hands tucked beneath my head the way I'd slept since I was just a little boy, I realized how true it was what Steve had said to me once. About how unfair it was that a fifteen-minute span of time could change an entire life, forever. There was no way of knowing when it would come, no way of knowing when everything that mattered would suddenly scatter like fallen leaves in a crisp autumn wind, or like ash from a fire.

All anyone could do, all *I* could do, was hold on to what mattered most with everything I had.

THE END

Mark P. Dunn is originally from Swarthmore, Pennsylvania but has lived most of his adult life in Ohio, Maine, and North Carolina, where he teaches high school English at small private school. Mark is married to the photographer Piper Warlick, and the two care for their daughters and for a veritable menagerie of animals, ranging from dogs to cats to chickens. Mark's first novel, *A Girl in Mind*, was published by Five Star Mysteries in 2006. His second, *The Last Night*, was released in 2016 by JournalStone Publishing. He has also published horror and suspense tales in various magazines and anthologies. Currently, he is at work on his fourth novel, a supernatural thriller set in the wintery woods of western Maine.

CPSIA information can be obtained
at www.ICGtesting.com
Printed in the USA
BVOW08s0210160218
508098BV00002B/155/P